When Joe Met
MATILDA

Belinda E. Edwards

Belinda E Edwards

Copyright © 2023 Sparkling Creatives

ISBN: 9798388182937

Sparkling Creatives.

Unit G7 Beverley Enterprise Centre, Beck View Road, Beverley, UK. HU17 0JT

Dedication

I wrote this story for you, my readers. It's my 'thank you' for your support as I wrestle with getting my stories out of my head and onto the page for you to read. Although I have written it for all of you, one reader requires a special mention, as she was very generous with her help to select the names for this one.

Thank you, Lynn.

for Susan,

Enjoy-

Belinda x

Chapter One

The Mediterranean glistened on the horizon as she took her first steps onto the yacht that would be her home for the summer. She wanted to stand and watch the waves toss the other yachts already at sea. They all seemed to dance to the same tune as the waves moved them to their own beat. Matilda wasn't here to admire the scenery, so when a grey-haired man with a beard pointed up to the bridge, that is where she went.

Excitement propelled her up the steps, but the heated voices inside stopped her from walking straight in. Instead, she knocked on the door and waited. She heard a grunt that sounded like 'come in,' so she did.

"Hi, I'm Matilda Sykes, but you can call me Tilly."

The Captain and the head steward greeted her with grim faces.

"I understand you have no experience of working on any yacht, let alone one this size. Is that correct?" Matilda shook her shoulders and offered them both a smile as she replied.

"Yes, but I'm a fast learner and I am here to learn."

"Have you ever been on a boat like this before? The last thing I need is someone still finding their sea legs."

"Yes, I've been on smaller crafts than with my dad."

"Your dad works on boats, that's good." Tilly didn't want to correct her. Yes, Maxwell Sykes did a lot of work whilst on boats, but Tilly couldn't imagine him ever being referred to as a sailor.

The woman who introduced herself as Zoe pushed a bag at Tilly.

"I'll show you your cabin." Matilda followed her silently down a tight corridor.

"Here you go, you are sharing with Bridget, get changed, then come and find me in the crew mess,"

When Zoe opened the door to a small cabin, Matilda stepped back. She couldn't believe she would share such a tiny space with another girl. She sank into the bottom bunk and inspected the contents of the paper carrier bag her new boss had given her. This was her uniform. Her wardrobe for the next twelve weeks.

Tilly wasn't sure what to make of the feeling in her stomach. It could be excitement or fear, but most probably both. What had she done? Why did she need to be so stubborn? *Couldn't I have proved how serious I am in an easier way?*

She gave herself a talking-to. Her friend Emily had been doing the same job since high school and had warned her the first few days would be tough. *If Emily can do this, so can I.*

With a deep breath, she pulled out shorts and a T-shirt, ready to find out what was on the list of jobs she knew would wait for her.

The dining area held a curious smell she couldn't place. Zoe was sitting next to another girl. Without looking up again, Zoe issued her first command.

"Bridget, I want the crew beds made and then the guest cabin beds. Start the laundry and keep rebooting it whilst you do all the beds. When you think you have done that, call me to check that they are all up to my standards."

The girl Tilly assumed to be Bridget didn't seem pleased until Zoe said,

"Take Matilda and show her what to do. She needs to know how to make a bed properly before the first guests arrive." Bridget smiled now. Zoe continued, taking pains to announce each syllable. "And Mat-til-da, after that I expect you to ensure we make each bed to that standard every day, and we wash the laundry to 5-star standards."

Bridget walked off to a panel in the wall, which she opened and pulled out clean sheets.

"You and I are sharing a cabin, Matilda, so let's start in there."

"Thank you, but please call me Tilly."

"Tilly?"

"Everyone does."

"Do they now!"

Once in their cabin, Bridget claimed the bottom bunk and set about making it. As soon as she finished, she sat down on her bed and pulled out a nail file.

"OK Matilda, let's see what you can do."

Tilly made her bed each morning, but she had never changed the sheets, nor had she put on a duvet cover. The staff did all those things at her parents' home.

She took much longer than Bridget; it made her companion sigh. Bridget excused herself to go reboot the laundry whilst Tilly changed both beds. When she had finished, she made her way to the laundry. She found Bridget sitting in the crew mess, talking to Zoe.

"Oh Matilda, there you are. Let me show you the laundry. You are going to be spending a lot of time in there, so it's best you find out how it all works."

By the end of the day, Tilly ached all over. She spent her first day cleaning, making beds and washing clothes. For the last three hours, she had been trying to iron the deck crew uniforms, including their white shirts and trousers. When she hung the last shirt neatly on a hanger, she proudly took it up to the Captain's cabin.

"So, Matilda, how was your first day? Has Zoe been showing you the ropes?"

"Well, I am tired, but both Zoe and Bridget have been really helpful. Thank you." Something in the way his lips curved told Tilly that the Captain knew very well how little they had helped her.

Zoe had been especially horrid about her bed-making skills in the guest cabins and had made her re-do the bed in the primary suite four times. Tilly had let it all roll off her shoulders. She doubted anyone on this yacht could be as exacting as her father. It might be arduous work, but for Tilly 24 hours without her dad, chipping away at her confidence felt like a holiday. This summer on the Mediterranean would be three months of not having to worry about living up to Maxwell Sykes' standards.

As she made her way back to the crew mess, she walked into a tall man around her own age. Tilly took in his tanned skin and sun-bleached blonde hair, together with his deck crew uniform. Every inch of this guy looked to belong on the deck of the Zeus.

"Hi, I'm Jake. You must be the new steward."

"Yes, I'm Tilly."

"Well, Tilly, you have five minutes to get ready for a night out with the rest of the crew."

Back in her cabin, Tilly walked into a cloud of what she presumed to be Bridget's perfume. Her legs ached, but when she undid the plait that constrained her unruly red hair, she realised her arms hurt more. The hours in the laundry had left her hair plastered to her body. She combed her fingers through her mane, leaving the curls cascading across her shoulders.

Tilly picked up her phone. Her finger hovered over her father's name a little too long, but what would she tell him? It wouldn't impress Maxwell Sykes that she had spent a day making beds. Tilly couldn't remember feeling so tired. Flicking open the phone case further, she checked that the card he had given her was still there. Her escape key, he called it. 'Use it when you want to give in, Tilly' she could hear the certainty in his voice. Tilly closed the phone case firmly.

A bang on the door reminded her she was supposed to be getting ready. She discarded the shorts and T-shirt and pulled on a simple blue dress. One more run through her long hair with her fingers and some colour on her lips.

Finally, up on deck for the first time since she arrived, she found Bridget and Zoe with Jake and another guy she assumed to be deck crew. His scrawny limbs and metal-rimmed spectacles only emphasised just how physically fit Jake was.

Before Tilly could introduce herself, Zoe spun on her heels and led off onto the shore.

"At Last! Come on, I don't want to be standing all night in these shoes."

Chapter Two

The morning sky threw out a myriad of colours as the sun sat just below the horizon. Tilly was the happiest at this time each day. Her duty started every day at six am, but guests were rarely that early. Zoe herself would not surface before nine most days. That in itself made Tilly feel lighter. She could get on with the list of jobs left for her without the constant jibes from Zoe or the twisted smiles from Bridget.

Instead, each morning the same routine. She ground fresh beans and started the coffee. With the pastries in the oven, she had time for her own breakfast. The scents in the galley each morning lifted her spirits. Today she took her cereals up on deck to enjoy the changing sky. She didn't get long to herself.

"Any chance of my coffee, Matilda?"

"Yes, Captain."

When she returned with his coffee, the captain smiled and, for the first time, didn't simply grunt his thanks.

"Thank you. So, six weeks in, how are you finding life below deck? Regretting it yet?"

Tilly smiled. The captain's frostiness reminded her of her father.

"Take a look at that sky. How could I regret that?"

The captain grinned and turned to leave. "And the work?"

"Let's say I will appreciate the hotel staff much more in the future, but it is getting easier."

Tilly returned to her tasks. Zoe had a lot of obscure ideas about table designs, but for breakfast, she left Tilly to her own devices. As she finished today's creation, the first guest arrived.

Zoe produced the jobs lists for the day as she and Bridget were putting away the last of the breakfast things.

"Today the guests are having a picnic at a cove up the coast. Bridget, you are coming along with me. Go pull out the tableware."

"Mat-Tilda!" Zoe watched once again for a reaction. When it didn't come, she snarled, "Go down and help the deck boys load the tender. Make sure they pack everything, including water, and towels. Well, even you should know by now what to pack, but I have made you a list! Do Not Fuck it up!"

Tilly dropped down to the swim deck, where she found Jake washing down the tender. Dave was trying to lift out the chairs and Tilly rushed over to help. If Tilly found it difficult to fit in, Dave looked like he would never find the physicality to be a permanent fixture on the deck crew. Tilly had seen George still trying to teach him how to tie the various knots.

"Here Tilly, let me give you a hand with that." The older man said when he found her attempting to carry a table on her own. Tilly smiled. Zoe thought sending her to work with the deck crew would be a punishment. Little did she realise Tilly would happily work on this team all day. At least she got to see some more of the sky.

Tilly re-rolled the towels and repacked the boxes for the beach set up carefully, checking everything off the list. Zoe hadn't listed sun cream or the first aid kit. Tilly packed them anyway. Finding the sun cream almost empty, she replaced that with a fresh bottle and added in the special sunscreen that the current guest had specifically asked for. *Has Zoe simply forgotten? Or is this another of her plans to get me into trouble?*

"George, will you check these? Have I missed anything?"

"Looks good to me Tilly, love. Are you coming with us today?"

"I doubt it," she laughed.

"Well, keep an eye on Dave, will you? Make sure he eats – and drinks – I don't want him passing out again."

"Sure, George."

"You know Tilly, you're a great bloke, really." This small piece of praise from George brought a smile to her face.

With everyone off for lunch ashore, Tilly could get on with the beds and cabins and, of course, the laundry.

With all the beds made, she called Dave down to the crew mess to eat. They shared some fresh chicken salad and some great bread left over from breakfast.

"Thanks, Tilly," Dave beamed as he slid onto the bench seat next to her.

"You're welcome. How's it going up on deck? Have you nearly finished?"

"You're hilarious. It's never done." He took a bite of his bread. Still chewing, he said, "How about you?"

"Like you said, it's never done, is it?" Tilly studied his face. "You look like you have been catching the sun. Have you got sunscreen on?"

"Well, I started the day with some, but I guess it's been hot."

"Put some more on – don't burn Dave."

They ate on in silence.

"This is nice, just you and me eating together. I find it overwhelming. Sometimes, I guess I don't speak at all. I let everyone else get on with it."

"I know what you mean."

"Tilly, is this what you expected it to be? Working on a yacht?"

Tilly laughed and tried not to spit out her salad.

"No, me neither."

"I have a friend, Emily; she's been crewing since she left school. She always has the most gorgeous tan, and she posts the most fabulous photos all the time. When I was slaving away at university, Emily's life looked so wonderful. I was so jealous."

"Is that why you came?"

"Part of it."

"There's more?"

"I loved University actually, but at the end of that, I wasn't ready to go back home. To all that means."

"I felt like that."

"Where is home for you, Dave?"

"Rossington, it's near Doncaster, you?"

"Harrogate."

"What's wrong with Harrogate?"

"It's not the place, it's…" Tilly stopped talking. This felt like the first genuine conversation she had ever had

12

with Dave. *Am I really going to talk about my family to him?*

"You don't have to explain if you don't want to, Tilly. It's OK I understand."

"It's hard to put into words, that's all. It's my family, well, my dad mostly."

"You don't like your dad?"

"Oh No! I love my dad but no one else does."

"OKKK."

"My dad can be a complete bastard. He is an exacting man to work for. My brother avoids him all the time at work. If he is hard on people who work for him, you don't want to know how hard he is on us."

"My dad doesn't even notice me, so I can't imagine that at all. I can't remember the last time we spoke. I guess I am trying to escape the nothingness of my old life. Deck crew seemed to be all I am qualified for."

After lunch, Tilly worked in the laundry, focusing on the ironing. On her own, she could play some music on her phone. It struck her how much quicker she could work now. Everything looked to be getting easier. Well, the jobs were. She still hadn't cracked the hard nut that was Zoe. And after six weeks, she wasn't sure that she ever would.

Chapter Three

"Tilly, what the hell are you banging about for? Have you forgotten there is no breakfast this morning?"

"Sorry, I am going now."

"What time is it, anyway?"

"5:30."

"5:30?"

"I like this time of day. I can get on deck before I start work." Tilly picked up her phone as it chimed.

"OMG! Who is that?"

"Probably my dad."

"Your dad?"

"This is his time of day, too. It's always the time I can talk to him."

Bridget screwed up her face. "You're weird. Most folks doing this job call their mum, not their dad, and they do that after work when it's been a shit day. Now you! You get up when you don't need to, to talk to your dad. Zoe's right. You're not right in the head."

"When do you talk to your dad?"

"I talked to my mum last week, or maybe the week before?" Bridget turned over, her back to Tilly, and the conversation was over.

When she reached the sundeck, Tilly checked her phone and found her dad's message.

DAD: Call me if you are up.

Tilly dialled the number and whilst she waited for him to answer, she hung over the rail watching the boat rocking in its berth.

"Ah, good morning and how is my favourite daughter?"

"Is everything ok, Dad?"

"Sure, sweetheart. I just wanted to check when you are going to be home."

"I finish here in two more weeks, then I go to Aunt Cecilia's in Paris."

"So, when are you home?"

"Dad?"

"Well, I've been thinking – about what you said last week – About working for me. If you want to start work here, I have some ideas."

"Brilliant Dad."

"Could you be home on Monday?"

"No Dad. I am committed here until the end of the month."

Silence followed by a sigh, as Maxwell Sykes said, "Tilly, you hate that job."

"I didn't say that."

"You didn't have to."

"I'm still going to see this out, Dad." Silence again, then finally,

"I guess that is what I wanted to hear. I don't want you working for me because you are not happy somewhere else."

"Dad!"

"I wouldn't want a quitter working for me."

"Honestly, Dad, you know me better than that."

"See you when you get home. Give my love to my sister."

"Sure, Dad."

"Bye Tilly." And he hung up.

Tilly had pondered what working for her dad would mean for so long, her coffee had gone cold. She took herself down to the crew mess to have a leisurely breakfast for once.

Zoe slumped down on the bench beside Tilly. Her sunglasses told the tale of yet another late night for the head steward. As Tilly got up from the table, Zoe groaned.

"Five today!" Zoe announced. Tilly had to assume the comment was aimed at her, as they were alone.

"Five?"

"Five guests. Parents and three sons. So, after you make the beds, set up a lunch table for five on the sun deck.

Tilly carried on clearing up the crew mess and made Zoe a coffee.

"Can I get you something to eat, Zoe?"

"You can do those beds, Mat-Tilda!"

"All done. I did them last night, whilst you guys were out."

Zoe groaned again and dropped her head onto the table. "An omelette–mushroom- and more coffee."

16

Whilst Tilly made the omelette, she made some toast as well. Better to get Zoe functioning again. If she felt rough, Tilly knew they would all pay for it. She hummed as she cooked, but stopped when she heard Bridget join their boss.

"Did you say three brothers?"

"Yes, I did, and if they are here with their parents, I'm guessing they're not married."

"Oh wonderful, that's one each."

"Well, only if we share with 'Call me Tilly'."

"I get your point."

Tilly paused with Zoe's breakfast in her hand. *Sod it, why did I sign up for this? What's wrong with wanting to be called Tilly?*

Fighting back her frustration, Tilly placed the omelette and toast in front of Zoe and handed her more coffee.

"I'll set that table now."

"And set up for five at the welcome table. Towels, champagne etc, well, even you should know what to do by now."

Chapter Four

As the tender carrying the new guests pulled alongside, the three dark-haired young men made the Cookson family stand out. Mr Cookson wore a light suit, whilst the wife wore a yellow dress covered in large red roses. Behind followed three jean-clad men that filled out their T-shirts well. Tilly could feel Bridget squirming next to her as she clutched a platter of canapés.

Zoe stood next to the captain, holding a tray with five glasses of champagne. Next to her stood a giggling Bridget. At the end of the line, Tilly was holding a tray of towels.

She didn't like how Zoe sniggered as the group approached. It distracted her as she studied the older man's face. Tilly thought Mr Cookson looked familiar. He introduced himself as James and then introduced his family. His wife Lynne. His oldest son, Patrick, was the tallest, with short, neatly trimmed hair. He held on to Zoe's hand a little too long for Tilly's liking, but Zoe seemed to enjoy the attention. The second son, Michael, was a little more relaxed, in both his hair and his dress. He had a wicked grin; something not lost on any of the girls. Bringing up the rear came Joe. His dark hair looked unkempt, as did the scruff that covered his well-shaped face. His clothes were clean, but she guessed his mum had something to do with that. He mechanically shook hands with the crew, with no smile on his face.

When he reached Tilly at the end of the line, she said a soft 'Hello' as he took her hand. Tilly immediately sensed a warmth she hadn't felt with the rest of the family. Joe must have noticed it too, because he paused and looked at her. Goose bumps ran up her arm. His gentle blue eyes held a sadness that tugged at Tilly. She couldn't remember seeing such despondency since she had arrived in Italy.

Joe was still holding her hand when Bridget nudged her. Zoe used her best 'I'm in charge' voice.

"If you would like to follow me, I'll show you the rest of the boat."

Joe offered Tilly a weak smile, then reluctantly followed his family to explore the yacht.

Tilly took the remaining canapés down to the lounge and went to the galley to check if she could help with lunch. Keeping busy seemed to be the right thing to do.

Tilly could hear Zoe laughing as she joined them.

"Oh, my God! That woman is so common, kept calling me love! How can they afford this?" She collapsed on the bench, holding her side. "Matilda, you can do lunch with Bridget. I'll choke if I have to serve them."

Serving the Cooksons came as a refreshing change. They acted like a normal family to Tilly. The older brothers were rather loud and joked throughout the meal. Joe, on the other hand, barely spoke. He sat at one end of the table and picked at his food. Staring at something off in the distance. Tilly struggled to look away from him. When Joe looked up from his meal and caught her eye, he offered her a small smile. It lasted a little longer than the first one. Tilly couldn't help but wonder what had brought the sadness to those beautiful eyes.

When they cleared the table down to the galley, they found Zoe sitting on the counter, drinking a glass of wine.

"What's the state of the laundry, Mat-Til-da?"

"I have everything washed. There's only the Captain's whites to iron."

"I'll do the ironing for you. Bridget and you can go with the guests. It seems 'Lynne' wants to go to a market! Seems she doesn't want to look at Louis Vuitton. She would rather look for a bag on a market." Zoe shook her head. "I don't understand these people."

Bridget giggled. "Patrick asked me if I could take them to a good bar."

"You just be careful, young lady. You should know better than anyone, not to fraternise with them after last season. I wouldn't want to lose you from the crew." Bridget scowled until Zoe continued, "you won't catch me playing kissy with the guests." Bridget laughed out loud. Tilly guessed this was another in-joke that she would find out about later because Zoe never thought to lower her voice. If she couldn't see you, she presumed you couldn't hear her.

"So go get into your white shirts and black skirts. And behave yourselves."

Both girls attempting to get ready at the same time in the one tiny cabin would always be a challenge. Tilly rushed to do the fastest change she could, escaping before Bridget started spraying her hair and using perfume. As a result, she was standing by as George brought the tender round. He looked shocked to see her waiting to board.

"My god! She's letting you out with the guests?"

"Yes, I know. Zoe is going to do the ironing for me."

"The ironing, indeed. Do you know, I think she quite likes to stay and do stuff like that now and then, especially as she had a late night? Whatever the reason, you enjoy it."

Mr and Mrs Cookson arrived on deck soon after Tilly. Patrick and Michael came next, followed by a flushed and giggling Bridget.

"Where's Joe?"

"I saw him going into his cabin, mum."

"Tilly, love, could you nip down and hurry him up? I'd send his brother, but somehow I think you will get a better response."

Tilly hesitated. If it had been anyone but Joe, she would have been halfway down the stairway already.

George nudged her, "off you go, girl. We need to be going before the tide changes."

Standing outside the cabin, Tilly paused again. This is silly. I just have to knock and tell him the others are waiting. Knock. Knock.

"What!"

"Sorry, your mum sent me." Tilly's hand sat on the handle. *Should I go in?* Before she could decide, Joe pulled the door open, pulling Tilly with it. She stumbled forward, falling into Joe.

"Tilly?" She pushed herself off his hard body. Staring down at the carpet. Anything but looking into those sad, beautiful eyes.

"Everyone is waiting to get in the tender. I think your mum wants to look at the market, and I guess your brothers want to find a bar." She mumbled, turning away.

"That sounds about right. Mum always likes to shop; that's how dad got her on this trip."

Tilly tried again. "They're expecting you, and I understand the tide is about to change."

"Can't I stay here with you?" Tilly turned back to look at Joe. He seemed so downhearted.

"Sorry, I have to go with the shore party."

"Why didn't you start with that?" He abruptly shut the door in her face. A little stunned, Tilly wasn't sure what had just happened or what to do next. Before she had time to think clearly, Joe yanked the door open again. He pushed his phone into the back pocket of his jeans. Tilly couldn't help noticing how well they fitted him. His face softened. *Did he see me looking? Shit!*

"Lead the way, Tilly."

As they climbed the stairs, Tilly became very aware of the size of the man behind her. He gripped the handrail, his body so close to her she felt a heat radiating from him. Tilly tugged at the hem of the short black skirt as she tried to climb faster, trying to put distance between them.

When they reached the deck, George started to load the passengers and crew into the tender. Jake helped Tilly down, lifting her as she stepped off the yacht. It made Tilly laugh until she saw the look on Joe's face. She sat down as quickly as she could, still rearranging the hem of her skirt. She tried not to look up. She didn't want to make eye contact with anyone.

She found herself sitting next to Lynne Cookson on a seat at the back of the tender.

"Tell me, Tilly, what will we find at the market?"

"I'm not sure, Mrs Cookson, I haven't been in the last year or so."

"First, call me Lynne, and you haven't been in a year?"

"It might be longer. It's unusual for me to go ashore with the guests. Well, I guess. But I have been here before with my family."

"How long have you been doing this? I mean, working on the boat?"

"Nine weeks, nearly ten."

"I see. Any reason you are joining us today?" George must have heard as he started coughing.

"Zoe, the chief steward, would normally come," Tilly searched for an explanation, "but I think she had other jobs to do." She didn't know what else to say. She blushed as she spotted Jake chuckling to himself at the helm. Tilly suspected he was the culprit behind Zoe's headache today.

Once ashore, George wanted to stay with the tender, and he asked Tilly to take James and Lynne to the market. The rest set off to explore the bars. To her surprise, Joe joined the shopping group.

Lynne chatted away as they walked down the narrow streets. The combination of being back on land and cobbled paths left Tilly feeling unsteady. When she rocked into Joe, he caught her. He held her arm as she straightened herself, blushing furiously.

"Sorry." It was mumbled, but Joe simply smiled back at her.

"Steady on love, don't go falling for that great lump."

"Leave her alone, James. I am hoping to find shoes and handbags. Do you think we will be in luck, Tilly?"

"Well, let's wait and see. Tell me what sort of thing you are looking for?" The two settled into an excited exchange about colour and how they loved the different styles of sandals. Lynne Cookson proudly told her about the jackets she had bought each of her sons the Christmas before. It filled Tilly's head with images of Joe Cookson in a butter-soft leather jacket. She felt her tongue flick out and lick her lips before she stopped herself.

Joe had fallen back and now brought up the rear with Mr Cookson. The market had mostly packed up. The food stalls were gone from the afternoon heat. The small square had cafes along one side. One stood out with its teal umbrellas and metal tables. People sat and chatted whilst waiters delivered coffees. Tilly was relieved to see there were still a couple of stalls selling just what Lynne had been asking about. Green striped awning sheltered the shoes and bags from the afternoon sun.

Lynne Cookson looked to be in heaven. Looking at first one stand and then the other, she was buzzing. She piled several sets of shoes and matching handbags together. James seemed pleased to see her happy, but Joe looked lost. It took the stall holders a long time to meticulously wrap each of Lynne's purchases. As they waited, Tilly stroked the sandals, excited by the choices. She picked up a pair of soft red leather ones and tried them on. She thought of her dad's credit card sitting in her room, but no! that was just what her dad expected her to do, spend the money on pretty things. She had her wages, but she hadn't thought to bring them. She carefully put the sandals back on top of the box.

James folded his wallet back into his pocket. "Tilly, love, I think Joe and I deserve a drink now. Can you find out where the others are?"

"Yes, of course." She pulled out her phone and wandered off to get a signal. She considered calling Bridget, but something made her dial Jake's number instead. Jake told her they had arrived at a new bar.

"Good news. Jake says they have moved to the Capri bar. It overlooks the harbour and has chairs and tables outside. I think you will like it."

Bridget was laughing even more loudly than usual. An assortment of beer bottles covered the table in front of her and the older brothers. The entire group appeared to be having a wonderful time. In fact, only Jake looked sober. He leapt up to go to the bar to fetch Tilly a soft drink. Lynne was on a high from her shopping and Mr Cookson just seemed happy to sit down and have a beer. Joe was the only one who looked uncomfortable. He took a bottle of water and went to hang over the railings watching the fishing boats. Tilly didn't like to see a guest look so unhappy. She started to get up to go and talk to him. Lynne stopped her, patting her hand.

"Don't you worry too much about Joe, love. In the last couple of weeks, he has drunk enough to last him a lifetime. I guess he has some thinking to do now."

"I had hoped he might enjoy the trip."

"I wish he could too. That is probably a bit too much to expect. I'm simply glad he came along. I couldn't have left him at home. Not drinking like he was."

Tilly tried to pull her eyes away from the hunched man with his bottle of water. Jake sat down next to her and began to chat. Jake had always been friendly, but then he was amiable with everyone. Tilly turned to look at him, anything to stop watching Joe Cookson in so much pain.

"So Tilly, is this a serious thing?" Tilly rattled the ice in her glass as she pondered her reply.

"Is what serious?" She took another sip of her drink, watching Jake over the top of her glass.

"I see you looking at that the one with a scruffy beard. And I notice he came with you, instead of drinking with his brothers."

Tilly swallowed hard and fingered the condensation on the outside of her glass. What did she feel for this man? He had certainly captured her attention, but there was nothing between them, nor could there be. She offered Jake a small smile.

"Do you seriously think I would fall for a guy with a scruffy beard?" Jake shrugged. She hoped she had done enough to put him off, but it had made her reflect on the emotions tumbling through her. *Why is it so hard to look away from this man? Is it so obvious? Why won't my stomach behave?*

Luckily for Tilly, Jake didn't get to push the point because a message from George announced it was time to go back to the Zeus.

On the way across to the landing dock, Tilly walked next to Jake. Bridget was giggling with Patrick and Michael, followed by their parents. Joe dawdled at the back, carrying the things from the market.

Zoe was waiting to greet them with a tray of mimosas for the guests. As Tilly stepped off the tender, she got her next instructions.

"You can help serve tonight. Bridget needs a rest."

Bridget looked like she needed a week of sleep, but it wasn't from work. Tilly wanted to remind Zoe she had been working for at least three hours longer than her colleagues had been up. She bit her lip; it stung that Zoe seemed to miss how hard she worked. It all felt remarkably familiar. Her father had the same problem.

His credit card was mocking her. She didn't have to do this. She stayed determined to finish what she had started. Only two more weeks.

Her legs and back ached as she turned down the beds. She left Joe's cabin until last. Stepping into his room, she stopped briefly to close her eyes and breathe deeply. With her palm flat on her chest, Tilly felt close to him.

On his bed, she found a shoe box. As she picked it up, a note fluttered to the floor.

For Tilly

For dancing on till morning.

Chapter Five

Inside the box were the beautiful red sandals she had been admiring that afternoon. Tilly's heart melted. It felt like the first kind thing anyone had done for her since she left the UK. She hid the shoes away in her locker, taking care not to let Bridget see the box.

Dinner was family style, and that meant less work for Tilly to do at the table. Instead, Zoe had her running up and down to the galley. Her legs felt like rubber, she had never felt so tired.

Mr and Mrs Cookson retired quite early, leaving their sons sitting at the bar in the lounge. They had been drinking most of the day but seemed ready to stay up all night, too.

Zoe stayed up to serve the drinks and sent Tilly down to bed, but not without warning her to be up for 6 am. Yet another niggle. She had not missed one early start since she joined, not that Zoe would know that.

At least she didn't have long to go.

In their cabin, Bridget was fast asleep and snoring loudly. Tilly tried to sleep, but it wasn't happening. She felt hot and kicking off the covers didn't make any difference.

At 2 am she gave up and took a blanket up on deck where, she hoped, there would at least be a breeze. She found the deck still and cool. There were fewer lights on the shore now, but they still look stunning as they climbed the steep slopes of the town.

She found a sun lounger on the dark side of the deck, looking out across the Mediterranean. She snuggled down under the blanket and closed her eyes.

"Did you find your present?" It was Joe's voice. She opened her eyes to find him standing over her. She smiled.

"May I?" he indicated to the lounger, and she shifted over so Joe could perch on the edge.

"I know this must seem bold Tilly, but I feel drawn to you. Tell me it isn't just me."

"Well…"

"I get it. I know it's silly. Perhaps it's a sign that I am over Alison, though."

He paused, but not long enough for Tilly to respond. Tilly watched his face, hoping he would explain without her asking. She needed to know more about Joe Cookson. She needed to understand why she was so drawn to him.

"We'd been engaged for six months. I thought I'd found my partner for the rest of my life and Alison said the same." He looked away, out into the darkness. "But what she actually meant was, hers until she found someone better, or do I mean richer, I'm not sure, really. It seems Alison was only using me to get into the sort of parties that people with money get invited to." He looked back at Tilly and took her hand. That heat flooded back, the tingle she felt when they arrived. "But when I hold your hand, I want to say Alison who?" Tilly still hadn't responded. She stared silently down at her hand encased firmly in his.

29

Joe bent his head and kissed her. His lips touched hers, still and gentle, until Tilly's body responded. The kiss grew, the heat grew, and Tilly moaned.

Her fingers reached into his beard and pulled him closer to her. His hand held her head. Her hair was down, free from the plait that was felt like part of her uniform. His fingers pulled through the length and swirled a curl by her ear. Only when the kiss stopped did Tilly process what was happening. Zoe's warning tripped a switch in her brain, and she managed somehow to jump to her feet, still holding the blanket. She clutched that blanket to her chest, trying hard to cover her half-dressed body. Joe stood up, too.

"I'm sorry. I thought you wanted this. I mean, the shoes and the hand-holding I thought you were as interested as I am." Joe rubbed the back of his head. "I'm sorry."

"No, I'm sorry I should have stopped you earlier. If I thought you were going to kiss me, I might have."

"You didn't want me to kiss you?" Rejection flooded his face and guilt filled Tilly's stomach. Her hand went to her mouth and her eyes went down to her feet. Frozen for a fleeting moment. Eventually, she lifted her eyes to search his face.

"Joe, you weren't in that kiss alone. I think you could tell that."

Joe grinned. "No, you did seem to be enjoying it." Tilly shook her head.

"But this is my job. If I had met you some other time or place, I would definitely not have stopped where that was going."

"Wrong time and wrong place? So, not the wrong guy?"

"I have only just met you, Joe, but no, I don't think you are the wrong guy. As I said, I can't do this now, here."

"Can we still be friends? I need a friend on this trip."

"As much as my job will let me, I would be happy to be your friend."

"Why are you up here, anyway?"

"It's hot in my cabin." She considered bitching about Bridget but decided against it.

"You don't have air-con?" Tilly shook her head. "You can always share my air-con." He said with a gentle smile.

"That might not be a good idea."

"So, what do we do now… as friends?"

"You have a busy day tomorrow. Maybe you should get some sleep."

"Not quite what I had in mind."

"Well, now I have cooled down, I am going to try to get some sleep myself."

Chapter Six

Tilly hadn't slept well. Bridget remained fast asleep on the bottom bunk. Her snoring was so loud that in the tiny space, the noise seemed to vibrate through Tilly's bed.

The way Zoe continued to treat her had started to get silly, but Tilly would not let it ruin her summer. What really kept her tossing and turning was the look on Joe Cookson's face. She replayed every conversation that had involved him since he arrived. His mother's comments about the fact he had recently been drinking heavily. She couldn't forget the sadness in the man's eyes.

Not sleeping when she should, resulted in Tilly oversleeping for the first time since she joined the Zeus. Bridget woke up though, and despite her having been in bed herself from 6 pm the day before, she made sure that Tilly got up by kicking at her bunk.

It was still before six am, so Tilly took her coffee and cereal up on deck to enjoy the sky. She might be tired, but she knew ten minutes up on deck before Zoe started on her today would reset her brain.

Finding Joe Cookson up there was a shock. Seeing him standing at the rail in just his PJ bottoms left her speechless.

"Oh!" was all she could utter.

"Morning Tilly, did you get any sleep after…"

"Not as much as I would like. Can I get you something?" Tilly's eyes were drawn to his naked chest.

He might not be looking after himself now, but at some point, this man had done some serious exercise.

"You should finish your breakfast first." His voice was soft and warm, and Tilly's resolve was slipping. She dragged herself to get back into work mode.

"I really couldn't eat another mouthful if a guest is waiting. So, what could I get you?"

Joe smiled at her but said nothing. Tilly's face flushed. She quickly realised that his pyjamas hid very little and now she could stop looking below his waistline. Gulping, she pushed on to get his breakfast order.

"The coffee is on; pastries will be ready soon and I can wake the chef if you want something cooked?"

"Oh God, no! Don't get anyone up. I am enjoying it being this quiet. Is there any more cereal? And coffee?"

"I guess there is cereal in the crew mess. What would you like?"

"Surprise me."

"And your coffee?"

"Straight white please."

"OK."

"And Tilly, will you eat with me?" Tilly had to fight to urge to reach out and touch this man. She licked her lips and shook her head.

"I'm afraid I can't."

"OK." Joe's voice was softer and sad now. Tilly felt guilty. He said he needed a friend, and she couldn't even sit and eat breakfast with him.

Tilly took her own bowl below deck and returned quickly with cereals and coffee for Joe. She took them over to the table.

"What happens today?"

"You're the guest. You get to decide." Tilly was hoping she sounded upbeat. She wanted every guest to enjoy their stay. But as Lynne Cookson had said, that might be a bit too much to hope for with Joe.

"My brothers won't be up much before lunch."

"The deck crew can set you up with a jet ski or some other toys?"

"Toys! What the hell am I doing here?" Joe dropped his head.

"Your mum said it was a celebration."

"That's what the meal is about tonight. It's a work celebration. We all work for the family firm. There is no escape."

Tilly could understand that. Joe took a spoonful of the cereal and looked up at Tilly.

"What else did my mum say?" Tilly could hear the concern in Lynne's voice when she talked about Joe's drinking. She shook her head.

"Nothing."

"Now that I don't believe. Was it something about me?"

"She is just concerned."

"About me?" Tilly didn't respond. What could she say?

Joe stood up from the table and left his cereal unfinished on the table. Tilly went about the rest of her jobs with her stomach in knots, remembering the pain in Joe's face.

As she moved up a deck to clean the lounge areas, she was so very much aware of the Cookson men playing with the water toys. The jet skis were particularly popular. The hum of the engines and the laughter filled the air as Tilly cleaned.

Joe looked to be enjoying himself at last and had started to relax.

Mrs Cookson found Tilly kneeling on the floor dusting the coffee table in the lounge.

"Ah Tilly, do you think you could make me a pot of tea? They do have proper tea, don't they? I don't think I've had a decent one since I left home."

"I can do that, Mrs Cookson. Where would you like me to bring it?"

"Please call me Lynne. I feel like my mother-in-law when people call me Mrs Cookson. If I sit in here, will I be in your way? They all seem to be enjoying themselves, but I just want to get lost in my book. I do love a good romance. Do you?"

Tilly thought it felt like a pointed question, but she simply smiled and went off to make a tray with a pot of tea and a cup and saucer.

Zoe found her in the galley.

"What on earth are you doing now?"

"Lynne asked for a pot of tea. I'm about to take it to her."

"Lynne now is it? Well, when you have done that, you take your lunch break. I am going to need you on service again today."

The meal that evening had been carefully orchestrated between Chef and Zoe. The captain would be dining with the guests, and that always seemed to create even more angst in the galley.

When Mr and Mrs Cookson arrived in the dining room, Bridget and Zoe began serving canapés and champagne. Zoe dispatched Tilly to start on the cabins.

"Be quick! We need everyone for service. Remember, the captain is joining them so in your blacks and back here as soon as."

The master suite was pretty tidy, and it didn't take Tilly long to get it ready. She could hear the boys bantering and she tuned into their conversation, ready to go do the same to their cabins.

"So, Joe, you are finally over that trollop, then. I saw you hitting on the crew."

"I'd give the redhead a miss if I were you. Zoe would be a better bet. I think she could teach you a thing or two."

"I can vouch for Zoe being a good bet."

"I was not hitting on Tilly."

"That's not what it looked like. Besides, I heard the redhead say she didn't like scruffy beards."

"You go for it, Joe. Go have some fun with someone who doesn't matter instead of getting engaged to the next gold digger who comes along."

"Patrick's right. The crew is there for our amusement. Enjoy it. Then go home. Plenty enough time for getting serious at some point."

"Hell, look at that expression on his face – he's falling in love – Again!" Tilly's heart was pounding as she bit her lip to stay quiet. Was he falling for her, too? She wasn't sure what she was feeling, but she couldn't stop thinking about Joe Cookson. And then she heard Joe's denial.

"Shit no! As you said, it's just a bit of fun." Tilly was sure her heart stopped beating in that moment. Her blood ran to ice. The three men made their way up on deck. Tilly had three cabins to sort, and she needed her face straight for service. As she worked quickly, trying to shake the feeling of betrayal, a single tear escaped. *Why did I think Joe was different? Why did I let him kiss me?*

Tilly took an extra moment when she changed into her black uniform to bolster her confidence. She brushed her hair and re-plaited it and slicked on some concealer to hide the shadows under her eyes.

The Chef had made a production over this the celebration meal of this trip. When Tilly arrived in the galley, he was plating steak and lobster. Jake and Dave were in their blacks too, ready to help get everything up to the table with speed.

More bottles of champagne were on ice for the extravagant dessert course that sat in the chiller. The amazing surf and turf had gone down well, and the family seemed relaxed and happy, even Joe.

When Chef carried the showcase dessert up to the table, the guests erupted into cheers. Even the captain looked impressed. Chef glowed as he cut and served his masterpiece onto plates for Bridget to pass around whilst Zoe opened and poured the champagne.

Mr Cookson insisted that another bottle be opened and for the crew to join him in a toast.

Mr Cookson stood up with his glass and addressed them all. Pride exuded from every pore.

"When my father started this business fifty years ago, I don't think he could ever dream that this," his hands waved at the table and the boat, "would be possible." He had to swallow before he could continue.

"I'm so proud of how well you have all worked this last year. This holiday, this celebration, is only possible because you have all pulled together to make the biggest deal ever. It might be my signature on that contract alongside that of Maxwell Sykes." *SHIT!* Tilly dropped the spoon she had been holding.

"But I could not have done it without all three of you. Here's to the next fifty years of JMC technologies."

Tilly felt light-headed. She bent over to pick up the spoon she had dropped and disappeared into the lounge.

She had managed for nine weeks to hide who she was. She wasn't about to let it out now.

Chapter Seven

The next morning, it did not surprise Tilly to find Joe up on deck again. She took him coffee and cereals and stayed up on deck whilst he ate. She itched to call him out on what he said to his brothers. But there was no trace of the entitled man she thought she had heard. Instead, the sad version of Joe Cookson sat alone, eating a bowl of cereal.

He looked up and offered her a weak smile and then, as he went back to mechanically eating, his eyes drifted away, and the sadness was back. *Is he thinking of that girl again, the one who dumped him? If he proposed, he must have loved her. So much for claiming he was over her when he kissed me.*

Tilly couldn't hold it in any longer. They were alone, so she braved speaking to him. Whatever he thought of her, a part of her hurt to see him looking like this.

"A penny for them – your thoughts, that is."

"50 Years!"

"I'm sorry?"

"You heard my dad last night, 'here's to the next fifty years'."

"Yes, I heard him."

"Well, what if I don't want to spend the next fifty years bending over backwards to do deals with men like Maxwell Sykes?"

Tilly's face dropped. She busied herself with setting up the rest of the breakfast buffet. Joe didn't notice. He still stared into his bowl.

"What if I have ideas for my own business? No one seems to consider that."

"You don't enjoy working with your dad?"

"It's not terrible. It simply doesn't inspire me. I'm the last one in the family to join the team. I will always be the youngest. I will never be able to change that, am I?"

"I think I understand."

"I doubt it." Joe shoved away his bowl and stood up abruptly.

"Thank you for breakfast. I hope I haven't brought down your day."

"I'm OK."

Joe stood in front of her, taking the time to study her face.

"You look tired Tilly."

"Well, thanks a lot."

Joe quietly left the deck, leaving Tilly on her own with so much going around in her head. She was sure she must have been asleep at some point, but the conversations of yesterday had kept her awake. No wonder she thought she recognised Mr Cookson; it was unlikely that her father had done business with someone he hadn't met several times. He liked to look into the eyes of anyone he did anything substantial with.

Eventually, the rest of the family arrived for breakfast, but Joe didn't reappear. The chef had the hot food ready to go to the table. Lynne insisted they should wait for Joe. She wasn't sure what would happen if she explained he already ate cereal. Chef certainly wouldn't be pleased.

"Tilly, love, use your charm. It worked before."

Tilly raced down the stairs, but at the bottom step, she stopped. Joe had looked so mad when he left the table earlier. The laughing voices she could hear were coming from the Master suite. Zoe and Bridget said they would do the cabins that morning. Tilly was just pleased to be getting more fresh air. As she stood in front of Joe's door once again, she froze.

"God, I wondered what use 'call me Tilly' was ever going to be. She is so useless."

"She does seem to manage to do the cabins and the laundry quickly."

"Do you think she will ever learn not to be so quick? I know I learnt that on my first boat. Don't work too quickly, you only get another job."

"I saw her out helping the deck crew yesterday."

"I know! She has no idea."

"At least she understands these guests. Their accents are so strong."

"How can they talk like that and be able to afford these prices?"

Tilly held her breath, trying to stop herself from bursting through the door to challenge them. Instead, she knocked gently on Joe's door.

When Joe opened the door, Tilly was more confused. In front of her stood a clean-shaven Joe Cookson. Her mouth opened, but no words came out.

"Could I ask you to check this bathroom?" He announced in a loud voice. Joe grabbed her arm and pulled her into his room, closing the door silently behind her.

Once they were inside, he let go of her arm and lowered his voice. Tilly rubbed her wrist.

"I'm sorry Tilly, but if I could hear those two, I'm guessing so did you!"

"Yes, well, please don't think we are all like that." She sank onto the bed without thinking. Realising the situation, she immediately jumped up and smoothed out and tuck in the sheets.

"I don't think you are like them at all. You're different."

Tilly's eyebrow shot up, but Joe smiled.

He reached for her hand and cradled it between his own.

"Matilda, Tilly, I don't care what your name is. You have a good heart, and you work hard. My cabin is spotless – but you may need to look at this bathroom."

Still confused, she opened the door to the bathroom. A smile broke out as she saw the problem. Joe had hair everywhere, clearly from shaving off that beard.

"Your family is waiting to eat! I'm not sure I can mention I gave you cereals. And now your mum is insisting you are there. I have to serve it, so the bathroom can wait. Come on. Chef will be doing his nut. He hates holding food when it's ready."

The voices in the other cabin had stopped. Joe reached for her hand, but Tilly shook her head. She hadn't worked so hard at sticking this out to be sent home. Sacked from her first job.

Joe looked sad again. And although it made her heart ache, Tilly could do nothing about that right now.

Tilly let Joe join his family, and she went to the kitchen to fetch the platters of hot food up to the sun deck.

At the table, the family appeared to be in a good mood and teased each other. Mostly, they seemed to be teasing Joe about shaving off the beard. Joe appeared to be smiling about it. Tilly tried hard not to look at him, and if she did, she seemed to catch him watching her. It surprised her at how that made her feel. She couldn't help smiling.

"Tilly, love, do you know where we are going for the picnic today?"

"Picnic? Oh, I don't know. George, the bosun, he'll know which beach you can get on."

"Can you find out what time we'll be doing that? Because I think the boys want to go on the jet skis again if there is time. I don't want them to make you late."

Tilly smiled; she liked this sort of consideration. Most guests just seemed to make demands from what she had picked up. And she wasn't used to being involved much after breakfast. She couldn't imagine that they would send her to the picnic. Two days off, the boat seemed too much to wish for.

Tilly cleared the breakfast table and found Zoe and Bridget making a big production out of packing for the picnic. Tilly nipped off to sort out Joe's bathroom before Zoe found it and blamed her.

The sink was a disaster area, with small curly brown hair everywhere. Just as Tilly thought she had them all, she would spot more somewhere else.

She was still in there when Joe got back. The door to the bathroom was closed, and Tilly wondered if she should make a noise so that he knew she was there. Then his brothers' voices were in the room too.

"So, brother, shaving the beard off, is that to please mother? Or is it because Patrick here told you that the redhead didn't like your scruffy beard?"

"I shaved my beard off because it was time."

"Time?"

"Time to move on after Alison threw my ring back at me as soon as she found someone with more money."

"You are well rid of the money-grabbing bitch; you do know she tried it on with both me and Michael, don't you?"

"Sorry brother, she only came after you once she realised we would never be serious about her."

"I can't believe you fell for it."

"Well, he is over it now and he can have some fun, probably starting with that Matilda girl."

They left the room together, leaving an angry Tilly to finish the cabins. She was hot and sticky, having already put in six hours of work. She could take her break when the guests had gone ashore. She had promised herself a long shower as soon as she could.

Back up on deck, Tilly could see they were almost ready to go. *Not long now.*

The thought had hardly left her brain when Zoe threw her another curve ball by sending her to pack the beach baskets. Fortunately, she was now in the habit of repacking them after every trip. *I'm going to soak my hair in conditioner, it's like straw now. Then I can reset my day. Things will be easier with Zoe gone, then she won't be able to keep switching my jobs.*

Down on the swim deck, Jake was putting the last of the food boxes into the RIB. Tilly passed him the beach basket after a cursory glance at its contents.

"Hurry Tilly, get in."

"Me? I thought Zoe or Bridget would be going."

It seemed Chef needs both Zoe and Bridget to prepare for tonight's dinner. That made little sense to Tilly, as Chef seemed to hate Zoe in his kitchen. Her disbelief was obviously clear to Jake as he continued. "I know, but who are we mere mortals to disagree?"

Tilly thought Jake liked Zoe, so now she felt even more confused. She climbed into the RIB with Jake still holding the basket.

George knew his job. He had found a spot that would please both generations. Jake set the table and five chairs on a rocky platform. George ferried the guests in pairs on the Zodiac RIB.

"Jake, give me a minute to freshen up. I was counting on a shower this morning once the guests came ashore,"

"You didn't share that with Zoe, did you?"

"Well, yes,"

"Fool!"

"Is that why I'm here?"

"That and she thinks these guests are beneath her. Rather like she thinks of me."

"I'm sorry Jake. I thought she liked you."

"She has fooled more than you. Your mistake is thinking that Zoe likes anyone other than Zoe."

The simple picnic looked delicious. Tilly felt annoyed with everyone, Zoe and Bridget and Joe blooming

Cookson and his cocky brothers. She stood with Jake to one side, but they were in full sun and Tilly was struggling. At Jake's insistence, she drank some water, but she wouldn't eat in front of the guests. She didn't even feel she could trust Jake anymore. Lack of sleep and food was taking its toll.

"I think you should get some sunscreen on, or there will be one more lobster at tonight's dinner." Tilly didn't argue. She walked quietly over to the beach basket for some sunscreen.

The bottle was empty. Tilly knew she had replaced an empty bottle with a full one only a few days before. Thankfully, Mrs Cookson had been keeping her family smothered in her own supply, so the guests weren't aware of the problem. Jake came over to Tilly. She was feeling dizzy, and nothing seemed to make sense.

"What's the problem? Do you need some help with that?"

"It's empty!"

"Empty… but I saw Zoe putting a new one in this morning." They looked at each other, recognising what that meant.

"I'll stand in the shade."

"You need to get inside, somewhere cool."

"Jake, don't make a fuss."

Joe must have seen something, because he shouted over,

"What's happening?"

"It's nothing." Tilly was quick to dismiss him, and her eyes pleaded with Jake not to say anything. Jake shook his head.

"Our sunscreen is empty. I think Tilly needs some." Lynne Cookson slapped her bottle into her son's hand, and Joe rushed over.

Joe opened the bottle and carefully applied it to Tilly's arms. Tilly stood there; her brain seemed to have stopped operating. Jake turned her round and Joe lifted her plait and applied yet more cream to the back of her neck.

"I don't think you have the best colouring for this sort of sun." Lynne Cookson had joined her son and began fussing over her.

"Tilly, love, why didn't you say? Come and sit in the shade."

Patrick stood up.

"Here, take my seat. Michael and I are going to walk down to that bar from the other day,"

"Don't wait up!"

"Patrick, look after your brother."

"Yes, dad."

Tilly hadn't moved, then slowly she curled and fell towards the floor. Joe scooped her up and sat her in a chair and lifted her legs onto another. Jake brought over some ice from the coolers. Tilly could hear their voices, but her eyes wouldn't open.

"I don't think she has sat down since six this morning." It was Joe's voice. *Why is he so concerned?*

"Has she eaten?"

"I doubt she has had time. She didn't finish her breakfast because I was up early. She went down to do the cabins after our breakfast. God! And mine was a mess!"

47

"Joe?"

"Sorry mum, it was shaving my beard in that tiny bathroom."

"Well, I should just be grateful you shaved it off, I guess. Now, what do we do about Tilly?"

"Does she need to go to a hospital or just go back to the boat?"

"Well, if we can't get her temperature down soon, I am going to say hospital. But let's try more ice and see if we can get her to wake. Somehow I can't see Tilly being happy if she wakes up in the hospital."

"Tilly, love, can you hear me?" Tilly's head contained all the voices, but they were going around and around in her head. She knew she needed to wake up. All she had to do was open her eyes. Joe's voice was the one she clung to most. *That bloody child. He's only using me. Why hasn't he gone with his brothers?*

Someone was holding her hand, and she knew that was Joe. Why was he there? Then she heard his voice.

"Tilly, Tilly, wake up I'm sorry about my bathroom."

"I'm pretty sure she hasn't passed out from cleaning your bathroom."

"Dad shut up. I just want her to wake up."

"Stop arguing. Look at her face. She can hear you."

"Should we put her in the recovery position?"

"Tilly, Tilly, can you hear me?" Joe's big hand stroked hers. She felt something cold and wet on her forehead. Tilly opened one eye and pulled at it.

"It's my handkerchief. It's clean." Joe chuckled.

"Thank God, now Tilly love, it's back to the boat for you. Jake, let's all go back."

Jake arranged for the RIB. Lynne insisted on travelling back with her. Tilly could tell George wasn't happy from the way he was growling at Jake.

Jake carried Tilly downstairs, with Lynne fussing behind him all the way. She insisted Jake carry Tilly to a guest cabin.

"Put her on Joe's bed. I will stay with the poor girl."

"Oh no, I can't do that. I will be ok, just let me lie down for a while."

The captain's voice bounced down the corridor. "Fetch some water and check the box in my cabin for rehydration fluids. Then let's get her in a shower."

"Captain, there is no room in here. Use Joe's cabin. The boys can share tonight if necessary."

"Jake, take her to the guest cabin. And get some ice. Then let's see what we can do."

Tilly was ready for the floor to swallow her up. All this fuss seemed so unnecessary. She had no idea what Zoe would say about it all. As she lay on Joe's bed with his mum firmly beside her, she realised she had no choice but to do as she was told.

Jake and Lynne stayed with her. Jake fetched a fan, and they set the air conditioning as low as they could get it. She was already feeling so much better. It was the Chef himself that brought her some food and Jake had set up a cooler of water and rehydration drinks. She could still hear Joe's voice hovering in the background.

With the air conditioning cranked up, Tilly soon began.

Chapter Eight

Tilly woke up in Joe's bed, his hanky still clenched in her hand. Her phone sat next to her. There was no sign of Joe or his mum. She lay still, her eyes closed again, letting her senses enjoy this moment of pleasure in a large and soft bed. She realised she couldn't hear any movement. Eventually, she heaved herself off the bed and went to the toilet. His bathroom had been emptied, but she could smell his minty body wash.

A knock at the door announced the captain, as he walked in carrying a mug of coffee.

"How are you feeling now, Matilda?"

"A lot better. I think I might have overslept. I'm sorry."

"Nonsense. The guests have left, so you're to take your time today. Take a shower after your breakfast, then try to sleep some more. There are no new guests until mid-day tomorrow so you can stay here until the morning."

When he left, the Chef came in with an omelette and another coffee for her.

"You enjoy a break today Tilly. I think you've earned it." This attention was new and made Tilly uncomfortable. But she did as she had been told.

She ate the breakfast and took a long shower in Joe's bathroom. Shocked at how drained that left her, she rested on his bed. Being there in Joe's space and in his bed stirred her emotions. For some reason, she felt safe there. What she didn't understand were the shifting feelings of what she thought of Joe. One thing she did know, she couldn't stop thinking about Joe Cookson.

Spending time in his cabin, she replayed the precious moments. The kiss, the early mornings, him holding her hand, the sad look when he drifted back to that dark place, the things she heard him say to his brothers. Mostly she replayed the time she was trying to sleep on the deck, the night he held her and, most of all, she remembered that kiss. Her lips tingled at the memory.

The next morning, Tilly rose early to start work. She started with cleaning and prepping Joe's cabin. Then she worked her way through the others. It wasn't unusual to find things left behind by the guests. Today the Cooksons all seemed to have left her something. In the master suite, she found a romance novel and some sunscreen. She found minty shower gel in Patrick's room. She wondered if it belonged to Joe or if all the boys used the same one. And in Michael's room, she found a business card with his mobile number carefully circled.

She remembered to drink plenty of water. By ten o'clock, she was taking her first break in the crew mess with Jake and Dave. Zoe rolled in and sank onto the bench with a groan. Jake made a coffee and pushed it into her outstretched hand. She mouthed a thank you and took a tentative sip.

"So, Ma-Tilda, are you ready to work? Or are we covering for you all day again today?" Jake sat down next to Zoe and frowned.

51

"Zoe, I know full well how often all of us have covered for you and Bridget after you have been drinking. Tilly was ill. It wasn't self-inflicted. But if you want to push it, we can get the Captain down here. I believe he would like to know why this happened."

"I'm ready to work, Zoe, and I will be more mindful of staying hydrated."

Once the new guests arrived, Tilly didn't see as much of Zoe. These were people that Zoe had served before, and she made certain she was always there. That meant that Tilly worked mainly below deck, cleaning and staying on top of the laundry.

Tilly was OK. She understood what was expected. If this was what she had to do to finish the season, she could do that. She took her breaks up on deck when Zoe went ashore with the guests. Bridget became much more friendly when Zoe wasn't around. Tilly was so ready for it all to be over. Paris and time being spoilt by her aunt were looking so appealing.

They had just one more day before the final guests arrived. Even Zoe was starting to relax. Jake and Dave invited all three girls to go out for dinner.

As the five sat around the table waiting for their food. Jake raised his glass.

"Here's to one last charter. Let's make it a good one." They all lifted their glasses to that idea.

Dave addressed the group next. "I'm not going back to the UK for a few weeks. I want to make the most of this weather. What are you guys up to?"

"I'm staying aboard," Jake sighed, "taking the boat across to Greece."

"I'm heading home to Dublin on the first flight."

"I think I might go to Paris. What about you Tilly?" The group fell silent for a split second when Zoe finally called her Tilly.

"Actually, I am on my way to Paris, too. I am off to stay with my dad's sister."

"Great, we can meet up!" Another stunned silence fell around the table. Tilly did not know how to respond to that.

Chapter Nine

Matilda Sykes stepped off the train at the Gare du Nord and out through the cathedral-like glass doors. She wanted to see and feel Paris. She wanted to walk in this city that she loved.

Her rucksack seemed bigger and heavier. She still carried that micro wardrobe she had left Harrogate with, and a few treasures she'd collected along the way. For much of the summer, she lived in her uniform and so her own clothes were hardly touched. Getting back into her own clothes was something she was looking forward to. It would be liberating. Wear what she wanted, get up when she like, and go to bed when she felt tired.

Her aunt Cecilia was her favourite of her father's sisters. The fact she lived in a fabulous apartment close to the centre of Paris was such a wonderful bonus. With no children of her own, Cecilia adored her niece, who she insisted on calling Matilda. For some strange reason, Tilly had no problem with that. Maybe Cecilia's French accent made it sound like another word.

The entire season had been intense. She had been adamant that she wanted this time away from her dad's shadow. She hadn't expected the work to be so all-consuming as it had been. Then, having any sort of job was new.

Tilly travelled in a large T-shirt and cut-off shorts. She felt as though she hadn't been able to get truly clean since she had climbed aboard the Zeus. Except, perhaps, for when she used the shower in Joe's cabin. Even after he left, that cabin was always his in Tilly's head.

Finally, after filling her senses with the joy that is Paris, she took the Metro out to the apartment. It was late. Her aunt would hopefully be out to dinner when she got there, and she could change before she saw her. Unfortunately, Cecilia had looked forward to Tilly's arrival and stayed home to greet her. It meant she was forced to meet her aunt, still in her cut-off shorts.

As she slipped into the chair at the small round table in the minute but immaculate kitchen, she smiled properly for the first time since the day Joe left for home. Isabelle, the maid, poured her coffee into the bowl-like China cup without question. Cecilia drank her coffee black, but there was cream in a pretty jug covered with tiny rosebuds.

"So pretty Matilda, where do we start?" Tilly held up her palm to stop her aunt, taking a sip of the hot black drink at the same time.

"Aunt Cecilia, I have no idea. I am just so glad to be back on solid ground." Cecilia grabbed her hand, horror written across her face.

"Your hands, my darling. I think we start with your hands and, quite probably your hair."

"Always start with the basics." They sang out together. Cecilia had told her as long as she could remember, 'attend to your hair and your nails, then buy good underwear'. Her aunt smiled.

"So, you listened. What I don't understand is why you look like this."

"This job made it all so difficult. There was no time for manicures or haircuts. Just washing my hair was hard enough. Rubbish water pressure in our cabin." She gulped down more coffee.

"Isabelle, we require double appointments for tomorrow. Ask if Philippe would be kind enough to style Matilda in the morning."

Cecilia's hair was an immaculate grey bob, and her nails were always the perfect French polish. Appraising her niece, she didn't stop.

"Now we must find something for you to wear. I don't think jeans will be suitable, even if you wear all of them." The tut was there. It was always there. "Can I lend you a dress, Cherie?"

"I have a dress."

"Excellent, bring it out for Isabelle to steam. I saw that bag you arrived with." The tut was there again.

"Thank you." With anyone else, Tilly would have felt upset at the tone of voice used by her aunt. The comments were a regular part of Cecilia's character and Tilly knew they simply showed how much she cared for her.

"Now, do we need to feed you before you go to get some sleep?" she pulled at Tilly's cheek. "I can't believe how bad you look. Has your father seen you?"

"No, not yet."

"Hopefully we can spare him a little then."

Isabelle took a salad from the fridge and placed it in front of Tilly. Again, she didn't ask or explain. Tilly ate the salad and enjoyed the glass of wine that Isabelle also produced. Cecilia sat next to her, but she didn't eat. She just talked and drank wine. She told Tilly all about the family gossip, who her sisters were seeing and who was going where, and with who over the summer.

"Where are you going next, pretty Matilda?"

"I'm going home."

"To Harrogate? What for, to open a tea shop?"

"I'm going to work for dad."

"It's worse than I thought. Mon Dieu. Tell me there is some handsome man back in Yorkshire who is pining away whilst you have been summering on the Mediterranean." Tilly laughed. At the words handsome man, an image of Joe Cookson minus his beard stood at the rail of the yacht in just his PJ bottoms. She blushed.

"So, there is a man. Where is this man?"

"No, my dear aunt, I am smiling at the description of me 'summering on the med.' I hope dad told you I was working. I was the third steward on a yacht. It's not very glamorous."

"My darling, whilst you are staying with me, you will excuse me for painting that brief flirtation with employment in the best light. What if we are introducing you to a future husband? What would he think? No, I consider it sounds better this way."

Tilly smiled. "I'm pretty sure my dad is saying the same, so I might as well get used to the idea."

"If I know my brother at all, I assume he will be immensely proud of how much you must have worked. But don't, for pity's sake, let him work you anywhere near as hard as he works himself." Tilly laughed out loud at the thought. "I don't think anyone ever works as hard as Maxwell Sykes."

Chapter Ten

When the sun rose the next morning, Tilly stretched out her limbs on the queen-sized bed. Just like making a snow angel, she enjoyed the sensation of space. She could feel the smile on her face, and it felt wonderful at last. Her hair was still a mess, and she had lots to do, but here in Paris with Cecilia to help. This was her coming of age. Her meagre wardrobe had been all she could manage on the yacht. Now, as she prepared to finally go home, she had more choices to make than what to wear that day.

She had been focusing so hard on escaping that summer. Then once she arrived on the Zeus, all she could do was concentrate on surviving all that the chief steward threw at her. Now here she was, twenty-two in Paris, with her whole life ahead of her. She had put so much energy into what she didn't want to do, now the time had come to decide what she was going to do.

At breakfast, Isabelle presented her with a black coffee again. She helped herself to cream and then started on the pastries that adorned her aunt's tiny table. Cecilia was next to her with her black coffee and her perfectly made-up face buried in the newspaper. Without looking away from her paper, Cecilia went through the day's appointments.

"Philippe is doing your hair this morning. I spoke with him last night. He wanted to see you before your manicure. So, we need to be there for eleven. You know I don't like to be late."

Tilly smiled. Cecilia was always late. She liked to make an entrance and that way everyone was ready when she arrived. In Paris, the whole family knew you had to live on 'Cecilia time'.

She had overloaded her croissant with black cherry preserve, so much so that it seeped out and onto her cheek. Cecilia passed her a napkin along with a look that would terrify a waiter at 50 paces. It was a look that made Tilly's heart sing because this was her aunt and she had missed her.

"Do we need to get you some fresh make-up, Cherie?"

"I have some with me." Tilly sipped the strong coffee and watch her aunt's face.

"Isabelle, call ahead about make-up. I have already spoken to my friend Caroline. She has an English daughter about your age, so she is meeting us to buy underwear later." Cecilia patted her niece's hand.

"Now, little one, go and get ready." Tilly looked down at her breakfast, still half eaten.

"You don't need to eat that; we will have lunch." Tilly obediently stood up.

"Fetch your dress first."

At the Salon Or Noir, a gentle stroll from Cecilia's apartment, Tilly filled her lungs with a heavenly perfume. Large vases of the deepest red roses perfumed the air but from somewhere lavender oils added to the atmosphere at this temple to beauty.

Sitting in a black velvet chair in front of Philippe, Tilly wanted to shrink. Ornate gold frames that held black and white photographs adorned every wall. Tilly couldn't put an age to the tall, dark-haired man who stood behind her. She studied his face, unable to decide if he wore eyeliner. Philippe ran his long fingers slowly and thoughtfully through Tilly's tousled hair, tutting, not unlike her aunt. Feeling the need to justify herself, Tilly stuttered out her excuse.

"I have been sailing in the Med for a few months."

"And you couldn't look after your hair?" Tilly bit her lip. She knew her aunt wouldn't want her to explain further. The sun and the salt added to the poor water pressure in her tiny shared cabin had all taken their toll on Tilly's hair.

"It's no problem for a man like myself. It is good you came today. Chloe will put a mask on your hair now and then after your manicure, I will transform this." He dropped the last section of her hair with a curl of his lip. He spoke in English, and so did her aunt. It was a relief, as her French was rusty. When she was younger and visiting Cecilia during the school holidays, she wanted so much for people to speak to her in French, and she thought she improved each year because of it.

When Tilly sat again in that chair, she had immaculate French polish with a delicate sparkle on both her fingers and toes. Philippe captured her hand and kissed it.

"Now princess, we add the crown you will wear every day." Standing behind her and looking constantly into the mirror, he lifted and dropped small sections of her hair.

"The colour is good. That is your good fortune, I think, little one."

60

Picking up his scissors, he began to sculpt a new shape into her hair. Adding layers and gently framing her face. He stroked her cheek with the back of his hand.

"You have wonderful cheekbones Cherie" Tilly blushed and said nothing. What could she say? Philippe carried on cutting and as he did, he carried on talking in English to her. His accent making each sentence sound like a song.

"Tell Me, Matilda, how long have you been in love?" He looked at her in the mirror, staring deep into her eyes, searching her soul. He stopped cutting, waiting for her reply. Tilly looked back. *In love? Am I in love?*

"It's new Cherie, now we have to help her win this man whoever he is?" Cecilia had arrived back in the room. She stood admiring her own immaculate bob in the mirror over Tilly's shoulder.

"But is this man worth this effort?" Philippe looked to Cecilia for the answer.

"Matilda would not love him unless he was."

"That is true." The Frenchman nodded.

"The better question is, will my brother find him worthy?"

"Madame, as ever, you are right."

Tilly sat still in the chair, listening to them discussing her with no wish to join in. Cecilia took a chair and picked up a magazine. The conversation was now over.

Philippe continued. The big sweeping cuts were over. Now he focused on the very tips of her hair, snipping tiny pieces. Stopping over and over again to comb out Tilly's hair with his fingers.

Chapter Eleven

A new text came in on Tilly's phone. It came with a photo of Joe's shaven face.

Joe Cookson: Are you back in the UK yet?

Joe Cookson: It's Joe.

Joe Cookson: Joe Cookson?

Tilly: I know who you are, just wondering how you are on my phone.

Joe Cookson: I added it when you were passed out on my bed.

Joe Cookson: SORRY.

Joe Cookson: Don't be mad, I couldn't say goodbye.

Tilly: So, this is you saying goodbye?

Joe Cookson: God No! I hope not.

Tilly: OK.

Tilly: Your face comes up with your name. Does my photo come up on your phone?

Joe Cookson. God no. I am not that big a creep.

Tilly: So just a little creep then?

Joe Cookson: Sorry.

Joe Cookson: So where in the world are you?

Tilly: Yorkshire.

Joe Cookson: That close?

Tilly didn't need to ask where Joe was. She knew where his family lived, and she knew she would see him soon.

Joe Cookson: Can we meet up?

Tilly didn't have any idea how to explain that she was the daughter of a man he despised. She realised it was something Joe needed to find out before anything happened between them.

Tilly: I'm not sure. I start my new job on Monday. I have stuff to do this weekend.

Joe Cookson: Can I ask again?

Tilly: If you want to.

She didn't type 'when you find out'.

Joe Cookson: I want to.

I want to ... The words echoed through Tilly's brain for days. Eventually, she asked for a second opinion. Emily was home, and they were comparing notes on the summer season.

"So, what are you going to do?" Emily asked as she passed the phone back to Tilly.

"I don't know."

"OK, different question. Do you like him?"

"God, yes, and I have no idea why." Tilly rolled her eyes and flicked back her hair.

"It's not because of your dad, then?"

"No, but is it something I should do? Have you ever met up with someone after the charter? Is it a good idea?"

"Is it a good idea? – NO. Have I ever done it? YES."

"And did it work out?"

"Do you think I would spend my Saturday morning shopping with you if I had a love life?"

Tilly looked away; she thought Emily was joking, but this time the joke hurt. She needed real advice today.

"OK." Emily paused and turned Tilly's head back to face hers. "Do I regret meeting up with these guys after?"

"Guys! Plural?"

"Yes, I have done it more than once. But the answer is No. I don't regret it because by seeing them, I worked out that there wasn't that much between us after all. Without all that sun and holiday spirit, there wasn't the same magic."

"So?"

"So, I say, meet him and find out for yourself. If you don't, you will always wonder."

"But my dad?"

"Why not message him back and see him this weekend, before you start working for your father? Then, if you like him, you can worry about this problem. If you don't like him so much, there is no problem."

"Do you think that will work?"

"Do you have a better plan?"

"I could wait until I've found a way to explain who I am?"

"So, he knows who you are. You go out, and it doesn't work out – awkward city!"

"I guess that's true."

"Tilly, go meet the guy. When you figure out how big an idiot he is, you can move on."

"What if he isn't an idiot?"

"Tilly, the man put his number in your phone … with his selfie photo. Who does that?"

"I was passed out on his bed, and he was leaving."

"And how many times did I talk to you about staying hydrated?"

"I know."

"So, message him."

"I already told him I was busy, and I start at Sykes International on Monday."

"You could say your friend went home early and left you in Leeds on your own."

"I guess that might work."

"Send the text. We can go look at shoes and if he isn't coming, I can stay."

Tilly: My friend cancelled on me, and I'm stuck in Leeds all day by myself.

Joe Cookson: Do you want some company?

Tilly: I wanted to check if you still wanted to see me.

Joe Cookson: Tell me where to meet you. It will take me 30 minutes, 45 tops.

"Where shall I meet him?"

"Try the Queens for lunch. You can make an excuse and jump on the train home from there easily enough."

"You've done this before."

"Tilly, some men have a personality transplant when they get back. I want you to be prepared to meet a different guy than the one you met in Italy."

With a resolute sigh, Tilly typed a new message to Joe.

Tilly: Could you make the Queens Hotel for lunch?

Joe Cookson: I'll be there by 12.

Tilly: Thank you.

Joe Cookson: No thank you.

"Now shoe shopping, I've seen some boots that had your name on them."

Tilly did love the boots and bought them, plus three new blouses to wear with suits ready for starting work on Monday.

Chapter Twelve

Tilly couldn't face sitting at a table waiting for Joe to arrive. A ball of excitement was building in her stomach as she remembered that first kiss with Joe on the deck of the yacht. She was worried about what Emily had said, that the guys were never the same when she got back home.

The tension in her body wasn't helped by the thought she would be hiding who she really was from Joe. Her brother had teased her all her life about her inability to tell a fib. She decided she would not lie. It wasn't like Joe was going to ask her point blank, 'are you the daughter of Maxwell Sykes?' *Well, if he did, it was probably because he already thought you were.*

After reapplying her lip gloss for the third time, she brushed her hair and flicked it back over her shoulders. She marched out into the main room and walked straight into Joe, standing in the doorway, shaking off the rain. His hard body was wet, and she stood back to take him in.

He was wearing dark wash jeans over brown boots, a navy sweater, and a chocolate brown leather jacket. His face was covered with the finest of beards, neatly trimmed. Certainly, a long way from the scruffy one he had been sporting when they first met. Tilly liked it. She found herself a little taken aback by the physical pull of this man now he was wearing more clothes. She had seen him in the smallest of swimwear, and that was an image she would not forget soon.

Joe dipped his head to gently kiss her cheek.

"Hello, Tilly. Am I late? Do you want to eat here? How long have you got?" Tilly smiled at the rush of words tumbling from this guy. "Sorry, I don't remember when I was more nervous. I was going to shave, but I thought I might cut myself. And! I know you don't like the beard."

Tilly reached out her hand and stroked his face. "This I love. The one you had on the boat didn't look like this."

"Yes well, mum has explained all that to me. Shall we sit down?"

They found a table for two near a window and picked up menus.

"How have you been Tilly?" He looked concerned.

"I was fine the next day. Sorry I didn't get to say goodbye. What about you? Have you shaken off your demons?"

"Yes, and No. Once I got home and bumped into the friend that Alison had left me for. Seems she left him after 6 weeks for another guy. After that, I realised it was always going to be over when she found someone 'better'."

"Better than you? Maybe I need to meet this friend." Joe looked sad until Tilly's face broke. "Only kidding," she laughed. And when Joe laughed back, Tilly started to relax.

They ordered food and chatted some more about Italy and his brothers. Joe told her all about the journey back from Portofino, and Tilly told him about Paris. Joe loved her new haircut, and she complimented him on the trimmed beard. He wanted to know about her new job. She kept it to the basics and said she would know more once she got started. His questions made her nervous, but Tilly couldn't remember the last time she had felt so excited on a date. *Is this a date? It's just lunch, right? He keeps holding your hand. Does that make it a date?*

Sitting and holding hands with Joe and looking at his face helped to make time fly by; the lights were fading outside, and Tilly decided she should go home before things went further. She realised if she wanted to see him again, she would need to explain about her family. He talked with such passion about how he was not enjoying work anymore and she thought much of that was the new deal with her father. She had to tell him, but she desperately didn't want to break the spell of this first date. *Again, with the date, this is not a date.*

"I think I am going to have to catch my train home."

"Let me drive you."

"Don't be silly, it's miles in the opposite direction." Joe frowned.

"How do you know that?"

"When I cleaned the cabin after you left, I found one of Michael's business cards."

"He does that deliberately, everywhere we stay. He thinks he might get lucky."

"Has it worked?"

"Not yet."

"So, I am going to catch the train."

"To where?"

"Harrogate."

"It isn't that far."

"From here, no, but then you have to drive back home."

"But I would have an extra hour with you in my car."

"It's not an hour."

"It could be."

Tilly collected her bags. "I have had a wonderful time. Thank you for saving me when Emily went home. I am going to catch the train now."

"Let me at least walk you through to the station."

"It's not that far."

"Humour me, will you?"

"OK." Joe helped her with her coat and then picked up her shopping bags. Walking out of the hotel, he took her hand. It felt so natural, and yet so special. His thumb stroked her palm.

"When can I see you again?"

"I don't know what to say, Joe. I start this new job on Monday. I probably should focus on that."

"Next Saturday, same time, same place?"

"Can I let you know? I'm not sure if I will need to work at the weekend." She blushed, trying to hide the panic she was feeling in her stomach. She didn't want this to be over.

At the ticket barrier, he put down the bags and took her face in his hands and for the first time, they kissed. A real boyfriend-to-girlfriend kiss. A feeling of being home washed over Tilly as their tongues danced together. And then, as if he had been practising it for years, he ended the kissing with a series of tiny kisses, lip bumps Tilly wanted to call them.

"Tilly, I don't want to let go. One last hug?" It was a big squeeze of a hug as he lifted her off the ground. Tilly laughed; Emily had been wrong. This wasn't as good as Italy this was so much better than that. It all felt so normal. She stroked his soft beard, tracing the neatly trimmed edges.

"You hate it, don't you? I'll shave it off."

"No, I like this one. It suits you."

"Till next week then." Tilly smiled. She realised she needed to find a way to tell him about her father, and until then, she would just have to work on keeping Joe at arm's length. If she saw him again, she would only fall more in love with this man.

The pull she felt as she walked down the platform and away from him forced Tilly to rub her stomach. It made her realise she was too late to worry about falling in love with Joe Cookson. It had already happened.

Sunday morning for Maxwell Sykes meant all the papers and gallons of tea. Tilly loved it. It was a special time she could enjoy with both her parents.

"Morning sister, you're looking all grown up sitting there with your black coffee and your laptop. Are you all ready for tomorrow?

"Hi Alex, what are you doing home?"

"Dad wants to talk; I'm guessing it is this merger with JMC."

"With you?"

"I do work there, you know, and so do you now. I guess it's time we talked about the ground rules."

"Ground rules?"

"Has dad mentioned it already?"

"Like what?"

"Like not calling him dad at work, you have to call him Max. Not Mr Sykes, not Maxwell, but Max."

"Why?" Tilly looked puzzled. Maxwell walked in from the garden room and answered the question himself.

"Because not everyone will know I'm your father and even those who do, don't need their noses rubbed in it. I ask everyone who works for me to do the same. 'Call me Max.' I must say it twenty times a day."

"See told you so. He believes people are more likely to talk to him. He doesn't realise how many of them are still scared of him. The guy who sits next to me calls him MMMax because he is so afraid of dad."

"So why are folks so scared of dad?" *Like Joe Cookson.*

"Pure reputation. He expects people to work hard, but no one works as hard as him. He's fair but he doesn't hang around if people don't fit, he moves them on."

"Does he use that voice at work? The one he used to tell us off?"

"Oh yes, if he gets annoyed with someone."

"I guess that's a few reasons, then."

"And now you're working in hospitality, under Janet Trench. You realise she has a worse reputation than dad. She doesn't have to fire anyone. They leave willingly."

"How is she worse than dad?"

"I'm not sure, but she changes her mind, a lot!" Alex paused, thinking before he continued.

"In fact, now you're working there, it's time I had another word with dad about that department."

"Why would you, in accounting, want to talk to him regarding Janet's section?"

"Would it shock you if I said because I look at the accounts?"

"Is that dad's plan? Plant us in various departments to check them out."

"Not directly, but he does use me to study various aspects of the company. Sort of auditing different areas to find ways we can cut costs without changing our outcomes. Looking at how and where we buy. Things like that." Max wandered back in and picked up another newspaper.

"Alex here, saved more than his salary, by simply sorting out how we buy paper." Alex beamed at his sister; praise did not come readily from Maxwell Sykes.

"Dad, why am I in hospitality?"

"I thought you liked the idea, planning parties and stuff. You're good at that."

"And Janet Trench?"

"Ah well, yes, now that you mention it. I need you to sit tight in there. Don't go blowing off steam if you see things you don't like. Watch and learn. There are two events to integrate JMC Tech into the family. I've told her I want you working on them. Anything you're not sure about, email it to Alex."

"Alex?"

"Yes, Alex. Janet knows you are my daughter, so she will be on the lookout for anything going to me. I'm not sure she has figured out Alex is family yet."

"That all sounds a bit like you want me to spy."

"It's not spying, I simply prefer you to give her enough rope. Don't let her know if you spot something. Not for now, anyway."

Chapter Thirteen

Joe Cookson: Good luck today

Tilly: Thanks

Joe Cookson: How are you getting there?

Tilly: I'm driving.

Joe Cookson: Be safe then.

Tilly tucked her phone into her handbag and got out of her car. It was 8 am, and she had been told to be prompt. A part of her felt sorry for Janet Trench, who must be wondering why she had Matilda Sykes in her department now. She had been running events for her father for as long as Tilly could remember.

She made her way to the first floor, where she found herself alone. She sat waiting until quarter past nine when the lift door opened. As Janet Trench swept in, she threw a blood-red pashmina over her shoulder. Renowned for wearing black, the red was her statement. She kept her white hair pulled into a tight bun. The lipstick matched both the cape and her nails. Dramatic in every sense of the word.

"There you are, Matilda." She said in a tone that suggested she had been looking for Tilly and not that she herself had just arrived.

"Well, come on girl, we were due at the hotel at nine am. You can drive."

In the car park, Tilly started rooting for her keys from the bottom of her bag. Janet stood spinning around, the pashmina swinging with her.

"Where is your car?"

"It's the white mini over there."

"Oh!" Tilly smiled inwardly at the shock on the woman's face. If she thought Max would spoil his daughter with a swish vehicle, she obviously didn't know the man or her. The Mini had been her brother's, and she inherited it from him when he bought a car of his own. Yes, her dad paid the insurance and made sure it was serviced correctly, but that was it.

"Hang on, I'll open the door for you it tends to stick a bit."

Janet's face contorted several different ways, until she said, "on second thoughts, we better take my car. I have things we will need in the boot."

They transferred to Janet's ancient Audi and arrived at the hotel over thirty minutes late for their appointment. They had to wait for over an hour for the manager to be available again because Janet insisted they couldn't possibly speak to anyone else but him. Tilly had to stop herself from rolling her eyes when she exchanged a look with the woman who had tried to insist they could talk to her.

The whole trip to the hotel took them out of the office until after three o'clock.

"Tilly, coffee in my office in ten minutes, dear. Angela will show you where everything is."

Tilly made Janet's drink black and strong like she had been instructed and decided she couldn't cope with any more caffeine herself.

"Leave it on my desk and take a seat." Janet didn't glance up from her screen. She picked up her phone and talked to Angela.

"I've read all the emails, dear. The answer is yes to all that. Just do what it takes. This event is super important. Mr Sykes will want everything perfect." Janet put down the phone with a flourish and turned in her chair to look squarely at Tilly.

"Now Matilda dear, I want you to understand, I say this with the most concern for you and your future at SI." Tilly cringed, her dad hated Sykes International being reduced to initials, and she wondered for a moment if she should share this with Janet.

"I have been working for this firm for over 20 years and I can tell you that you need to think about what you wear. Stick to strong basics, classic colours, and classic cuts. Forget all this fashion following you are trying to do. Get some simple white blouses to wear with your suits." She stopped to offer Tilly a patronising smile. Aunt Cecilia saying get the basics right sprung to mind, but Cecilia had been very clear about her finding colours that suited her better than black.

"Well Thank you, Janet."

"Mrs Trench."

"Thank you, Mrs Trench."

"Well, off you go. Go get back to your desk." As Tilly got up to leave the room, Janet had to add that last little dig.

"Oh, and Tilly, be on time tomorrow." Tilly could feel herself going red, biting her lip as she remembered what her father had said.

"Thank you, Mrs Trench."

Chapter Fourteen

Joe: How was your first day?

Tilly typed several answers, never pressing send. In the end, she sent one word.

Tilly: Exhausting.

Joe: Don't be working too hard.

Tilly: It's difficult when you are new.

Joe: I need you fit for Saturday. I have plans!

Tilly: I'm pretty sure I am going to be working. SORRY.

Joe: If you don't want to see me, just say.

Shit, I want him to know about dad and say he doesn't care. I just can't tell him yet.

Joe: I thought you enjoyed Saturday.

Tilly: It's not an excuse. I do want to see you again.

Tilly: Let's make plans for the week after.

Joe: Same time, Same place?

Tilly: It's a date.

Joe: A real date? Can I take you home this time?

Tilly: Yes Joe, you can take me home.

Joe: Do you have a place of your own?

Tilly: No, I moved back with my parents after Uni,

Joe: So, will I also be meeting your parents?

Tilly: If they're home.

Joe: Well, you've met mine & my brothers, so I have nothing to hide.

Shit, Shit Shit! Tilly threw her phone down on the kitchen island. It knocked into her glass of wine and sent it tumbling to the floor.

"Something wrong Tilly?"

"It's nothing mum, I forgot someone's birthday." The lie made her blush.

"You've had a lot on your plate. If they are a friend, I am sure they will forgive you."

Tilly cleaned up the broken glass, anything but think about the mess she was creating. Eventually, she picked up her phone and carefully typed a reply.

Tilly: I want you to meet them.

I want you to know he isn't such an evil man.

Joe: Is that good?

Tilly: I think so.

Joe: Early night then?

Tilly: Yes, I think it's going to be a long week.

Joe: I wish I could tuck you in again.

Tilly: You tucked me in?

Joe: Do I sound creepy if I say I still remember you lying in my bed?

Tilly: No, I remember waking up in it, sad that you were gone.

Tilly: I didn't think I would see you again.

Joe: I had hopes.

Tilly: Joe, I'm glad you put your number in my phone.

Joe: I was hoping you would ring me.

Tilly: If I knew I had your number, I might have done.

Joe: Only might?

 Joe: Tomorrow can I ring you?

 Joe: So, I can hear your voice.

Tilly: I'm planning nothing but work.

Joe: Until you see me.

Tilly: Until I see you. Can you ring after seven?

Tilly: And not too late.

Joe: That I can do.

Tilly: Goodnight Joe.

Joe: Goodnight.

Chapter Fifteen

Tilly had been at the hotel since 6 am. She wanted to say she had been up early, but the truth was she had not slept at all. She had been tossing and turning, trying to find the words to explain about her dad. It didn't help that all week she had been picking up just how hard and exacting he could be at work.

It had been a painful process for Tilly. To see this other side of her father. She, more than anyone, wanted him to see how hard she worked. She couldn't bear the thought that he would assume she hadn't put everything into this event.

And then there was Joe, beautiful, wonderful Joe. He had called and texted all week and been so supportive of how hard she worked. Maxwell Sykes had been down in London looking at the next acquisition, so he hadn't been there to see any of it. All he would see were the things that she felt sure would go wrong today.

And last of all, her boss, Janet Trench. Her dad had said 'sit tight and watch'. She had been sneaking things over to Alex, who hadn't replied to any of her emails. He had sent her a cryptic text message that said something about he was looking forward to seeing her at the next family meal and thanking her for her present.

Tilly hated the way Janet worked. She hated the way she treated the people who worked in her department. But Janet was a product of how her father had run his company for years. His exacting standards and his low tolerance for things that he didn't consider were right.

From what Alex had said, Max clearly recognised things were wrong in Janet's section. So why had nothing been done?

By 10 am the guests were arriving, and Tilly felt flustered. Despite all the time there had been to prepare, the team was still rushing around when they should be greeting people.

Someone had rearranged the badges on the table in a wonderful pattern. Only now they were no longer in the alphabetical order that Tilly had spent so much time doing. Queues were backing up as more and more people arrived. She bent over the table, trying to sort them out. She could feel the heat in her face as she got redder and redder. She had abandoned her jacket in an effort to keep her cool.

She hadn't seen the Cooksons arrive. The first she knew was when an angry Joe grabbed at Tilly's arm, turning her around.

"Tilly, what are you doing here?" Tilly wrenched her arm away from him. Having been arguing with him and her dad in her head all night, she felt so angry with them both.

"What does it look like?" she snapped.

"It looks like you are working for Maxwell Sykes."

"There you go then." Tilly blew her fringe off her face.

"Why didn't you tell me?"

"I would assume that was obvious, Joe. You made it perfectly clear what you thought of him." Tilly had kept her eyes on the job in front of her, but now she looked earnestly at Joe.

"If you got to know him…"

"And have you got to know him in one week? I bet you've only seen him at a distance."

"Have you ever spoken to him Joe, this man you are so certain is evil?"

"A week Tilly – what can you learn about the man in a week?" Tilly looked back at her hands, working mechanically, sorting the badges. How could she begin to explain this? As she hesitated, Joe's brain filled in the gap.

"Oh, my God! Tilly, you knew this man before you started this job." A queue behind him got louder as Joe searched her face.

"Is there a problem, Matilda?" Janet's piercing voice made Tilly jump.

"Joe, I will explain, just not now. I need to sort this."

Joe turned and left with his badge clenched in his hand. Tilly tried to breathe again. She had little hope of being able to talk to him today. She went back to the mess of the badges until her father stopped her.

"Tilly, your mum says you didn't eat breakfast. What time did you leave home?"

"Max, not now, please."

"I'm not even sure you ate yesterday. Where were you?"

"At the office." Tilly's face coloured up again.

"Not with this new guy, the one your mum wants me to find out about?"

"Not now, please."

"What were you doing at the office yesterday?" Tilly nodded toward a stack of gift bags at the end of the table.

"I had to gift wrap every item for 300 gift bags. Janet insisted you like everything 'properly wrapped'."

Maxwell Sykes shook his head. "Don't worry Tilly, all this is going to get sorted out soon. Give it a month. And email Alex."

Once everyone had arrived, she felt able to circulate the room more. Matilda didn't plan to work at Sykes International all her life. Part of her desire to work for her father was the opportunity to meet those people who made things happen in the business world. Still a little uncomfortable talking to people on her own, she walked over to Alex, who stood with a small group near the bar.

She smiled at Alex, hoping he would introduce her, but she didn't need to worry. As soon as she got close to the group, a tall, well-dressed man spotted her and, holding out his hand, introduced himself.

"A new face at one of Maxwell's events. How refreshing. I am Jackson Wilde, but my friends call me Jackson. I hope you are going to be a fantastic friend." He took Matilda's hand and kissed it. Matilda's skin bristled. "This is Alexander, the son of our host." Jackson Wilde pointed to her brother.

"The smile on your face just now tells me you've already met. Do not let him fool you, he's only the accountant of a rich man. I am the real thing. I could make that smile of yours so much brighter." Exchanging a look with Alex, she withdrew her hand.

"Well, Mr Wilde, you are right. I have met Alex before, and I can assure you I know him very well. And I am quite aware how boring accountants are," she laughed at her brother. "I much prefer Mr Sykes Senior."

"Stop it Tills. Jackson, may I introduce my sister, Matilda Sykes."

"Oh, a feisty woman, I do love someone with a bit of spunk. Do you have to stay long, or can I tempt you away somewhere far more interesting?"

"I am here to work, Mr Wilde. Now, if you will excuse me, I am probably needed elsewhere."

For the rest of the morning, Tilly kept pretty busy doing silly jobs for Janet. She could see Joe and the rest of the Cooksons working the room in the same way her father was. As it approached time for the buffet lunch, Michael took the time to come over and speak to her.

"Fancy seeing you here Tilly, not quite as sunny as your last job."

"Good morning Michael."

"Tell me, what have you done to throw Joe back to the dark side? If he starts growing that beard again, you only have yourself to blame."

"I have done nothing to your brother, other than start my new job for a man he hates."

"We could find you a job with us if it would put a smile back on Joe's face. He has got more work done in the last two weeks than he has in the four months since Alison left him." Tilly's eyes instinctively found Joe across the room. It was the first time she had seen him in a suit, and he looked good. No, it was more than that. He looked like a man who belonged in the suit that fitted him to perfection. It showed off his broad shoulders and strong thighs. Tilly remembered how strong his arms were. Joe Cookson looked great until you looked at his thunderous face.

"I have a job, Michael. Joe needs to learn that Maxwell Sykes is another human being. He has high expectations, and he gets things done."

"He gets things done alright and yes; we wouldn't be working with him if he didn't. Joe's a big softy, really." He touched Tilly's arm. "Give him a chance."

"Matilda, can you go sort out that buffet?" Janet certainly seemed to pick her moments.

"I hope Joe will listen when I have time to talk to him, but right now, I must work."

Despite all the meetings with the hotel team, or maybe because of them, there seemed to be some confusion about the day's menu, and Tilly found herself left trying to sort it out.

She tried pulling emails up on her phone to show the manager who said they could sort the problem but it would cost extra. It was the same old message. Janet swanned over and waved a well-manicured hand.

"Yes, whatever it takes." The manager smiled and walked away.

"Does that happen often?"

"What Matilda dear?"

"That we have to pay 'whatever it takes'?"

"I am sure you tried to do your best, dear, but your father will want this done right. Don't worry, I won't tell him you messed up." And with a swish of her black chiffon dress, she waltzed off. Hovering around the room like some black and white butterfly.

Tilly had run out of patience. She hadn't eaten and could feel her head starting to swim. She made the decision to take some food and a bottle of water and sneak off to the bedroom the hotel had let them use. It held all their bags and equipment. She needed to eat and decompress before she blew a fuse or passed out again.

As she put her hand on the hotel room door, she heard Joe's voice.

"Tilly, I'm sorry. Do you have a minute to talk?"

"Oh Joe, I'm sorry. I just didn't know where to start." She opened the door. "Come and keep me company."

But as soon as Tilly stepped into the room, the ground came up to meet her. She dropped her plate and the bottle of water.

"Not again Tilly." Joe swooped her up into his arms and laid her on the bed. In his panic, he phoned his mum to come and help.

Tilly started to come around to find Joe holding her hand as he sat next to her on the bed. Mrs Cookson stood at the foot of the bed, smiling.

"Don't worry Tilly, I've spoken to Mrs Trench, and she is getting you some food. It would be nice if you stopped doing this."

Joe softly stroked her hair. "Tilly, please tell me you will leave this job. You've been working silly hours since it started."

"Joe I can't. You don't understand, you see..." She still felt woozy and struggled to find the right words. Joe passed her the bottle of water. But before Tilly could explain, the door burst open to reveal a furious Maxwell Sykes.

"Sweetheart, what happened?" He sat on the bed, holding her into his chest. Joe recoiled. He stood up and staring down, saw his new love in the arms of a man he detested. When he saw Tilly curl into this devil's embrace, the pain in his chest became simply too much. He never considered Tilly would be like Alison, dumping him when someone richer came along. He had foolishly believed that they had something. From that first handshake when he walked on the yacht. He had lost his heart to yet another money-hungry woman. Patrick had tried to warn him back in Italy, but he hadn't listened.

Lynne Cookson tried to explain, "I think she has gone too long without food and water again."

"Again?"

"She collapsed on the beach in Italy. She was fine after a good rest, food and plenty of water. But as this is the second time, I would suggest you get it checked out."

Tilly had lost consciousness again and hung limp in her father's arms. He lifted her from the bed.

"I'm not sure how you know all this, but thank you. I am taking her home and don't worry, I will get to the bottom of this."

Tilly's eyes fluttered open, and she looked up for a moment at her father's face. "I'm so sorry Max."

"Don't worry sweetheart, I'm taking you home."

"Hmm, yes, take me home." And her eyes closed again.

"Is this why you defended him? How long has this been going on?" Tilly's eyes flew open.

"Joe, you don't understand."

"Oh, I understand all right. I thought I loved you, Tilly. I can't watch you with this man. I don't care who you are, Mr Sykes. You can't treat your staff this way. I realise in some convoluted way I work for you now, except I don't. I quit."

Joe stormed out of the room as Tilly shouted to him, "Joe, come back!"

Lynne Cookson followed her son out of the room, her face ashen.

"Where's Joe gone?"

"I don't know, sweetheart. Let's get you home. But I think first you better try to drink some water."

"OK, but Joe, why did Joe go, dad? You must speak to him."

"First, we need you sorted. Anything else can wait. Ah, Alex, thank God. Can you get some food and more water?"

"Sure, but what happened with Joe Cookson? He just stormed off muttering something about you being an adulterous dinosaur."

"Really?"

"Now dinosaur I get, but have you really been playing around behind mum's back?"

"Don't be absurd, son."

Alex laughed as he looked at his sister curled into her dad's chest. His arm lay protectively across her shoulders as she tried to sip more water from the bottle.

"Did he, by any chance, see you cuddling the latest member of the hospitality team?"

"Shit! He already thinks you are a monster and his last girlfriend left him when she met someone richer." Alex and Max looked at Tilly.

"Tilly! spill little sister."

"I met Joe in the summer. We had a connection from the day they arrived. Nothing happened, well there was this one kiss and. . Then when I passed out, they put me in his bed… no cad … he moved out to sleep with his brother and wher I woke they were gone."

"So, you haven't seen him since Italy."

"I didn't say that."

"OK Tilly, you can tell us the story later, but right now I think we nave a bigger problem. Even if no one else heard what Joe Cookson said as he left, his family heard him. Dad you need to nip this in the bud now."

"First things first, son. I better explain to Joe."

"Dad let him go. He has been so pig-headed about you and if he can expect so little of me, then, well … just let him go."

"OK sweetheart, drink."

"No dad, remember how many people out there are thinking something already. This sort of news will spread."

"Is it true what they say about no publicity, being bad publicity?" Alex shook his head.

"Dad, it's time for your speech to welcome JMC to the family."

"Of course, and are the rest of the family still here?"

"Yes, but here is no telling how long they will stay."

"Are you OK Tilly?"

"I will be." She stood up. "See, I am better already."

"Is this why we lose so many staff?" Alex asked.

"Maybe she does what she believes needs to be done, son."

"It's all so unnecessary, dad."

"Here drink, if you can stay long enough for me to get through this speech… Alex, get her some food? Do I even want to know why you were in this bedroom with that man?"

"Will you two focus? You drink. You straighten your tie. I am getting food, then we get this speech done." When Alex left, Max turned to his daughter.

"So, is this the guy?"

"Dad! Don't misjudge him. He is a good guy."

"Misjudge him? The guy who tells me to shove my job?"

"I like him."

"Tilly, how many people do you think have the nerve to do that?"

"You might admire him, but if he sees you, I mean us - well, to even start to assume that you would – for him to consider that I would do that, then maybe he isn't the man for me. Let him go."

"I have to try to save this deal. They will forfeit a lot of hard cash if they try to get out of it. I can't have people thinking…"

Alex returned with food and orange juice.

"Someone said a sugary drink is the quickest thing, so drink this."

"How do you feel now? Do you think you can do this? We can't simply let them walk away."

Tilly stood up and Max passed her another bottle of water and took her hand. Together, they walked to the stage. Tilly could see Patrick and Michael in a heated discussion. James stood to one side, looking quite stunned. There was no sign of Joe or Lynne.

"Ladies and Gentlemen.

"We are here today to celebrate that JMC Technologies is now part of Sykes International. I hope you have enjoyed today's event. I am particularly proud because Sykes is a family business, the same as JMC. And that is why I am happy to work with a united family like the Cooksons.

"Today is special for my family too, as it is the first event that Matilda, my daughter, has been involved with since she joined the business last week. So welcome on board Tilly. I am proud of how hard you work."

Tilly's eyes were trained on Michael and Patrick. It was Michael who reached for his phone. Tilly prayed it was to let Joe and his mother know what he had just heard.

As Maxwell stepped down from the stage, he squeezed Tilly's hand.

"I want you to go home, but I think I need to talk to the Cooksons. If you don't want to wait, I can get someone else to take you."

"I guess I should come with you to speak to them. We need to try to give him a way back in, dad."

"I know, sweetheart."

The conversation with the Cooksons went well. Tilly hoped it was a good sign. James Cookson was very apologetic, but Patrick and Michael seemed to find it all funny. They all tried to explain that the issue with his last girlfriend had done more damage than anyone realised. It had left Joe second-guessing everyone.

Maxwell made it clear that if Joe wanted to come back, it wouldn't be a problem. James wasn't so sure.

"Until he calms the hell down, he can take some unpaid leave. Tilly, I am sorry you were unwell again. I hope you get that sorted. I expect the best thing we can all do is give Joe some time.

Lynne will be worried, so would you please speak to her even if you don't speak to Joe again?

And congratulation this was a great event."

"Again, you are welcome. But I hope the next one ends better." Max offered a rare smile to James Cookson.

Chapter Sixteen

It felt like the longest week Tilly could remember. Max had insisted that she take Tuesday to rest and get a thorough check-up. Her iron levels were down, but the doctor didn't seem worried. She did feel that Tilly's lifestyle needed attention. She talked to her about the hours she worked, getting some good sleep, and eating properly. The doctor had been most insistent about her staying hydrated.

Back home and with her feet up, she called Lynne Cookson.

"Hi, it's Tilly."

"Oh, Hello Tilly love."

"James asked me to call and let you know I had been to see the doctor."

"Did they find anything?"

"No, I just got a telling-off for going without stopping to eat."

"So, Maxwell Sykes is your father. I guess working hard comes with the territory."

"How's Joe?"

"Embarrassed, he does like you Tilly, that's why he reacted so extremely. It's been a rough few months for him. I don't think he has any idea what he wants from life. The others, well, they are so driven, I'm sure you understand."

"It made me so angry that he could believe that about dad, about me."

"He knows that. Are you still upset?"

"I don't know, not as much as I was, I guess."

"Tilly, love, please don't mess with him. I'm not sure how much more he can take."

Alex came for dinner. That didn't happen often, and Carole Sykes had pushed the boat out. Max arrived home early and wanted all the details.

"Max, can't this wait? Let Tilly get herself back to normal before you go on a witch hunt."

"Mum, there is one more event with the department heads from JMC. It is essential that is not another mess."

"The thing I need to figure out is, does Janet create the opportunity for these people to charge what they like, or is she part of it?"

"And how will we work that out?"

"I really don't know, son."

"This next event is important. Would you let me take over that? It would give you some time to watch her some more?"

"Matilda, I need you to rest and get well."

"I can keep it simple, but maybe this is a chance to do something different. Janet has made all your events identical, and so they become indistinguishable."

"Do I take it you have an idea?"

"I might."

"So tomorrow we can talk about that."

"So sister, what about the youngest Cookson brother? Have you been in touch with him yet?"

"No."

Her mother patted her hand. "Tilly, sweetheart, I would like to know a little more about this young man."

Tilly told them that the Cooksons had been charter clients, and how she felt attracted to Joe despite the scruffy beard. She explained the story of his girlfriend dumping him. She was certain that would be a key factor in why he had been so quick to jump to conclusions when he saw her with her father. Tilly tried carefully to add that Joe already had a poor opinion of Max.

"I'm sorry, dad. I believe that if he took the time to get to know you, he would like you better. Sadly, I don't think he can see a future working within the company."

"I am not about to go soft, Matilda."

"I'm not asking you to change, Dad."

"I won't stop you from seeing him, but I don't want you to worry about this."

"I honestly have no idea what I am going to do about Joe."

"Maybe you do what James suggested, give him some space."

"Well, we have a date set for Saturday lunchtime."

"Tilly, will you think about this carefully? A lot of work went into setting up this deal. What dad isn't saying is, this could get messy when you stop seeing him."

Tilly had been going around in circles with this since that first date. Well, probably since she heard Joe talk about her father with so much venom. It hadn't helped her find an answer. Until Alex suggested there would come a day when she would stop seeing Joe.

She had imagined so much. Worrying about what sort of future they could have together. Listening to that one sentence, answered a lot of questions for her. Tilly could not imagine a world where she didn't want to see Joe again.

"It might be a good idea if I go up and get ready for bed. I have a lot of catching up to do. I need to be back in the office to sort this event. It's next week, isn't it?

"Did I say yes to that?"

"Go on Dad. I can't help but think Tilly will come up with something a lot more fun than anything Janet's got planned." Maxwell Sykes looked at the faces in front of him. Only when he was sure his wife would not kill him for saying yes did he agree.

"My office on Friday morning with Janet. Tell me the plans."

"Thanks, Dad."

Tilly almost skipped upstairs. She dived onto the bed and rolled onto her back. She could do this. She could help Joe see they would be good together. She would make them all see that.

She grabbed her phone and dialled Emily.

"Em, have you got any free time this week? I need your help."

Chapter Seventeen

On Wednesday Tilly went into work. She had one thing to do: put a plan in place for this next event. She wanted it to be something different from the corporate clone events that Janet created.

Talking to Max, she realised he needed the meetings to be more memorable. He wanted the department heads of the two companies to get to know their opposite number. He had given her the go-ahead to change things up.

Tilly decided to take them out of the offices and hotels, out of their suits and into jeans and bowling shoes.

She produced the structure of a small tournament where each department head would be paired with their counterparts. She had to contact Michael Cookson at JMC to talk over some details. He sounded super excited about the idea and seemed to think that JMC would win. He appeared to miss the part about each team having a player from each company. Tilly smiled to herself because all that would be clear come the day. She needed shoe and shirt sizes so she could have everything ready when they all arrived.

"So, Tilly how are you? Have you heard from my brother?"

"I'm fine, thank you, Michael, back in the office and sorting this for next week."

"And Joe?"

"He sent me a text yesterday."

"Just a text? The boy's a fool! If you are looking for someone with a bit more brains and much better looks, you have my number."

"I'll be in touch with the final details."

"Call me, anytime, Tilly."

When she ended the call, she studied her phone and looked one more time at Joe's texts.

Joe: Tilly I'm an idiot, please forgive me. I realise that this has to be the end for us. Your dad will never get over what happened. Tilly, I did love you.

Joe: No. I do love you, that's why I am walking away.

Tilly didn't tell Michael she hadn't answered the text. How could she?

She had promised her mum she would leave the office at five on the dot and she only went over by ten minutes.

But when she slid into her Mini to drive home, she had a plan in place.

She found Alex waiting for her at home with a pile of boxes.

"What's all this?"

"Mum is so not happy with you going into the office today. Dad told her that his daughter was too headstrong for him to even try to stop her. He had me call down to central purchasing and pick up this gear so you can work from home."

"So, I can't go to the office?"

"Yes, you can, but now you can also work from home."

"OK. Can we set it all up?"

"We? You need my help with something?"

"Probably not, but it will be quicker with your help."

"You realise you can't use this equipment for making TikTok videos and all that social media stuff?"

"Shut up, brother."

"So, where do you want it?"

"Good question."

Chapter Eighteen

Her mother persuaded Tilly to work from home on Thursday, and it wasn't such a bad idea. She could wear her comfiest jeans and one of her uniform T-shirts from the Zeus. She pulled her hair into a high ponytail. No make-up today.

By the time Emily arrived, she had the timetable for the tournament laid out. With a week to go to the event, everything had to go to the printers as soon as she got the final go-ahead. Emily had a brilliant eye for design, so together they worked on the look of the day. Tilly had a list, and one by one, they crossed off the designs as they were completed.

Shirts for each team. Players' surnames on the back. Although Tilly loved the fact that there were three shirts with Sykes on the back and three with Cookson on, it disappointed her that Joe wouldn't be there.

"Tell me again why there is no shirt for Joe?" Tilly tried to explain it to Emily. She knew the theory. She didn't like it.

"His dad has insisted he takes immediate leave. From what Lynne said, I think James blames himself for not helping Joe deal with this earlier."

"So, what are you doing about Joe?"

"I'm not giving up, that's for sure."

"This isn't you just being stubborn Tilly, is it? You know what you're like when someone says you can't do something."

"God! I hope not."

"Well, what is it then? I warned you things change when you come home."

"But that's the thing, Em. If anything, the attraction was stronger when we met again. I love the way he makes me feel, and he makes me smile. Even as I was passing out, hearing his voice helped me feel safe."

"I can't help but wonder if it's what Alex said. A challenge from Alex has always pushed your buttons."

"I don't have the words Em, it's a feeling in here." Tilly thumped her centre. "In here is a pull. It's physical. My body has to move toward his body. I need to touch him, his face, his arm, anything."

"I'm guessing there is a plan in Tilly's brain."

"I'm still going to the Queens hotel on Saturday."

"What if he doesn't turn up?"

"Then I have to think of something else."

"Can you get him to this day that you're planning?"

"A Plan B, you mean?"

"Yes Plan B, pass me those shirt designs. Let's make sure your shirt works for you."

"I guess mine should be the same colour as Janet's. She is my department head."

"OK, we can do that."

"Can we also work on Plan A, too, whilst you're here? Help me decide what to wear."

"I haven't seen all your buys from Paris yet. We could do a wardrobe audit, so you have outfits for Plan C and Plan D."

"Shit, do you think I will need Plan D?"

"No, but it would give you outfits for some dates when Plan A works."

Tilly looked down at her check-lists.

"We better get through this lot first and then I need to present this tomorrow."

"Do we need clothes for that, too?"

"Of course."

When the alarm went on Tilly's phone, the girls took a lunch break in the kitchen. Only when they had gone through Tilly's presentation for the next day several times, did they start on 'project wardrobe'.

Tilly wanted to start with an outfit for Friday's trip to Sykes International HQ. She pulled out her black suit and black heels. She paired it with one of the simple white blouses she had bought following Janet's lecture.

"I prefer the blue suit it's got a great cut but can't you find a top with a bit more ..."

"Colour? Pattern? Style?"

"Yes, yes, to all of that. What about the ones you bought in Leeds?" Tilly showed Emily the tops she originally bought to go with the suit, and they chose one.

"Hang on to that green one, the one that wraps over." Tilly waved the blouse on its hanger.

"Yes! try that one with your jeans and those boots I made you buy."

"I'm not sure dad would consider that this is a good work outfit."

"But what about your lunch date on Saturday?"

The girls laughed and played for two hours. They got as far as sorting through Tilly's underwear. Emily seemed impressed with all the Paris buys, and they were both trying them on when Maxwell Sykes arrived home. He came up to the bedroom to see what all the laughing was about.

"Working hard, daughter?"

"Always Dad."

"Everything ready for tomorrow?"

"Yes, just thinking about what to wear."

"I think you might find that a bit cold."

"Good tip, father."

"I have a message for you from Michael Cookson. He says they have a change to one of the teams." Max read from the post-it note in his hand. "Swap Alison Parkes for Joanne Hansom and the new shoe size is 8."

"Well, I guess your timing is impeccable I am about to send the shirt order through."

Emily stayed for dinner, and when she left, she hugged her friend.

"Stay strong Tilly. Let me know how Saturday goes."

Chapter Nineteen

The wine she had drunk with Emily meant Tilly had finally slept soundly. As she slept, she didn't dream of all the hurdles that were keeping her and Joe apart. No last night, she had dreamed about that first kiss on the Zeus. She drifted through that lunch at The Queens hotel and that wondrous kiss at the ticket barrier. She dreamed about Joe carrying her to bed. Her brain replayed waking up in his bed, surrounded by the aromas of Joe Cookson. Throughout those dreams, the Joe Cookson with her was the one in dark blue jeans and a neatly trimmed beard.

Tilly's stomach turned relentlessly on Friday morning, not because she needed to present to her father, although that made her nervous enough. Her biggest concern came from offering an untried event in front of Janet Trench. She had toyed with the idea of dressing according to Janet's clothing code. Life seemed pretty confusing at the moment, and she had to stop trying to please everyone.

She wore the blue suit but with a red fine knit jumper. Then paired it with the red sandals that Joe had left for her. She took a photo of her feet and sent it to Joe.

Tilly: Wish me luck

Joe: I'm not sure why you need it, but you always have my best wishes. The shoes look good.

Tilly: I love them, thank you. See you tomorrow. Same time, same place. X

Joe: Tilly, not tomorrow.

After switching it to silent. Tilly slipped the phone back into her bag. She made her way to her father's office.

"Come in Tilly, do you want to do this in here, or shall we use the conference suite next door?"

"The conference suite. I want to do this properly."

"Go get yourself set up. I have plenty to do until then."

Tilly was adjusting the screen when Alex arrived.

"Good morning Tills. Wow, you're looking good today. Is this from Paris?"

"Yes, well, everything except the shoes. Joe bought them for me in Italy."

"So, there was something between you guys out there?" Alex took off his jacket and sat down.

"There wasn't really time, but we did connect, though. There is just something about him. I don't know why, but I feel this pull to him." Tilly banged her hand into her solar plexus.

"You remembered what I said about all this Tills? It could get messy." Tilly's anger fired up her face as she snapped back at her brother.

"If we break up! Only if we break up!"

"OK! I'm sorry, I'm sorry." Alex held up his hands in surrender.

"Now what?" Tilly shrank back at her father's voice. "I could do without Janet seeing you two bickering. Alex, you are here for moral support."

"I thought I was here to ask questions about money?"

"Yes, yes, you are. Is this something I need to know about?"

"No." the siblings answered together.

They were saved from further questioning with the arrival of Janet Trench. She had dressed in her trademark black with the big red pashmina across her shoulders.

"I hope I'm not late. I have been waiting for Tilly at our office." She flounced into the room. "I haven't seen her since Wednesday, I couldn't be sure."

Tilly couldn't control her eyes rolling and Alex nudged her under the table.

"I'm sorry Janet, I did send you an email about that yesterday morning."

"That will be Angela not telling me again."

"Well, we are all here now, so can we get started? I'm sure we all have other things to do."

"Yes, of course, da... Max."

Alex smiled at his sister. It took him years, and he still hadn't made the switch to Max.

"I chose something active for this event, something that would mean the companies working together and getting to know each other."

"The hotel is the obvious place. They keep all that outdoor team-building things, Matilda."

"Yes, and our team has done the same things for the last four years." Max sighed.

"I agree, which is why I arranged for us to have a ten-pin bowling tournament."

"A what?"

"A tournament I will pair people up, one from each company, to play in a competition." That made Alex's eyes sparkle.

"Competition, what's the prize?"

"I ordered trophies, but we could add something extra?"

"I guess that depends on how well you did with the budget."

"Can we come to that later? It's one of my last slides."

"Can you email me the figures, Tills?" Janet's face didn't move. Tilly pushed on.

"I've teamed people up with their counterparts. It will give us eight teams." Her slide showed the names of the heads of departments from each company.

"That's a lot of matches."

"I plan to play in two pools of four teams followed by playoffs. I booked four lanes out for the day.

"We will eat lunch after the pool games. After we eat, the minor place play-offs will happen on three lanes and then the final on its own so everyone can watch.

"You and Mr Cookson will do the prize giving." Tilly paused for their reactions. She watched her father's face the closest.

"People need to want to win Tills, a plastic trophy isn't enough."

"Holiday, an extra five days off in the next 12 months."

"Mr Sykes' that is very generous." Janet clutched her pashmina.

"It's only five days for each firm. I'd better check with James, though."

When the costs came up, Alex was quick with the questions.

"Do you have a contingency budget?"

"I was struggling to see where I would need one, but yes, I kept some back."

"Who are you working with at JMC?"

"Michael."

"He's the pretty one?"

"Michael is the middle son."

Janet sat blankly in her chair; she started fidgeting with the collar of her blouse.

"Max, I know you wanted all the heads of department there, but I really think Matilda could use the experience of stepping up for this one."

"I will be there, Janet, working with the venue and keeping things moving."

Chapter Twenty

Saturday arrived at last. Tilly couldn't help but worry. Plan A was the one she had the most confidence in. The first time they met at the Queens hotel was the best time they had spent together. No arguments, just lots of laughs and smiles. It made Tilly's face ache all the way home on the train. And the kisses, they had been wonderful. If Joe could remember how good it was too, then she was sure they would be back together in minutes.

She had promised Joe he could drive her home, so she took the train in the carefully planned outfit. The thirty minutes it took to get into Leeds seemed to stretch today. Tilly wished she had driven anything but having to sit still for so long.

She pulled out her phone and took a photo of her boots and sent it to Joe.

Tilly: So, you recognise me.

Joe: I would know you anywhere.

Tilly relaxed a little. That looked like he was going to turn up at least. She started to see a future. If she could see him away from work, she could persuade him they would be good together.

Her nerves were still twisting her stomach. She dived into the toilet when she arrived to make sure she looked her best. She stood in front of the mirror, adjusting the wrap front of the blouse and her hair. She picked up her lip gloss and paused. *What if he kisses me? Of course, he will kiss me.*

When Tilly saw Joe hunched over the same table they had shared two weeks ago; she lost all her confidence. Sad Joe was back. He didn't look like he was there on a date. He looked more like he was waiting for his execution.

"That's not a good look. Should I just walk away now and save you the trouble of whatever you want to say?"

"Tilly no, you have to let me apologise and explain."

"I'm not sure I have to do anything of the kind." Even as she said the words, she heard James Cookson saying they needed to give him space, but it was his mother's words that made Tilly sit down.

"Thank you."

Tilly didn't want to look at Joe. One glance at his face had told her everything she needed to know. When he took her hand in both of his, she looked away. *I will not cry.*

"Tilly, you need to let me explain." She didn't want to hear it.

"Does that mean I get to explain, too?"

"Tilly, if I walk away from working with my family… well, I do not know what that is actually going to mean finance-wise."

"Do you think that bothers me?"

"I have a lot of thinking to do, and I need to find myself first before I can even begin to contemplate sharing my life with someone else.

"I'm damaged, Tilly. Being dumped has left me seeing problems even when there aren't any. My response to seeing you with your father is only one example.

"I care about you far too much to put you through all that."

"Did you ever consider I might have a mind of my own Joe Cookson?" Joe's eyes smiled.

"I believe you are the strongest woman I have been fortunate to meet. I could love you, Matilda Sykes. In another life, I would be fighting to keep you. But I can't do that." Tilly looked away.

"Tilly, come outside; I want to show you something." He stood up, still holding her hand, and gently pulled her out of the hotel and onto City Square. Tilly followed him. She thought she would follow him to the moon if he asked.

He took her to one of the statues.

"This is John Harrison. Much of this city centre, Briggate and the surrounding streets, were owned by John Harrison. When I look at this statue, I see a cold hard man who never married. He didn't have children and when he died, his estate was set up in trust for his sisters' descendants." He squeezed Tilly's hand.

"My Great Grandma was one of those descendants and because of that connection, my grandfather who started JMC had some of his education funded by the trust. He and then my father have been very successful.

"I do not want to be like John Harrison, cold and hard."

"How do you know he was cold? Because he is a statue?"

"Tilly, please believe me, I thought this through."

"Do you think he was cold because he didn't have children?"

"Tilly, that's not really the point. I wish I could make you understand."

"He might have loved and lost. Have you thought of that?" She pulled his hand. "Joe, this is history. Your life is your life. You are young! You can do whatever you want to do."

Joe shook his head.

"Tell me, Joe Cookson, why do you think you can't live the life you want?"

"Because I am expected to join the business. Look at you, working for your dad. It's what families like ours do."

"Just because someone is holding a door open for you doesn't mean you have to walk through it!"

"Tilly, I don't have the words to explain how I feel about you, about us. I do know right now I am messed up. I don't want to hurt you, so I know I have to walk away."

Tilly threw her arms around his neck. "Stop talking. I can't hear this."

"Tilly please." She seized his face and kissed him. Anything to stop the words that she didn't want to hear.

Joe hugged her so hard. Tilly knew he didn't want to let her go. The hug went on. Neither of them wanted to stop it. Tilly couldn't hold the tears back any longer. When the first sob left her body, Joe pulled away.

"Come on. It's time for me to drive you home."

"You don't have to do that."

"Oh, I do. I need to apologise to your dad, too."

Tilly stopped crying and swallowed. "You might not want to do that."

"I have to do that for my family."

"I get why you think it could be necessary, but honestly, my dad thinks you're great."

"Why?"

"Because you stood up to him. If you go apologising, there is a chance he won't respect you the same."

"Come on. You're right, I really don't want to do this, but I have to. Just like I must let you go. It is something I must do. The sooner we get started, the quicker it will all be over."

Tilly pulled away.

"Fuck you, Joe Cookson! Neither I nor my father need you, so you can piss off!"

He caught her arm and turned her around. "Tilly no, please. Don't make this any harder." Tears streamed down her face.

"Tilly, I can't let you go home on the train."

"But you can drive away when you get there!"

"Tilly, please, I don't want to hurt you. Please stop crying."

"Oh, what did you expect, Joe? That I would say thank you, Joe. Thank you for saying you love me and then saying you were walking away to save me?"

This was not what Tilly expected. She thought if she could just get Joe to admit he cared for her, and she got him to understand that her dad sort of liked him already, everything would be OK. She had imagined them driving back to Harrogate laughing, holding hands, and making plans. Right now, she wasn't sure she was ever going to recover from this man.

"Come on Babe." Joe put his arms around her shoulders and steered her down a side street. Once they were away from the crowd, he stopped and handed her a handkerchief.

"Another one for my collection?"

"Collection?"

"I still have the one from Portofino." The words came out between sobs.

"You see. I make you cry. I'm not going through life making you cry. I can't be the reason you are unhappy."

They reached his car, and he put her in the passenger seat and closed the door. He ran round to the driver's side and realised she hadn't fastened her seat belt. He reached across and did it for her.

"I have to keep you safe."

"What's the point?"

"Oh Tilly, I don't want to hurt you, I seriously don't. You will understand one day." Tilly sat next to him, staring out of the window, silent tears spilling down her face.

"Twelve months from now. We will bump into each other, and you will thank me for setting you free."

"Are you sure, Joe?"

Joe reached and squeezed her thigh before taking her hand and squeezing.

"I know how much I cried over Alison."

"Have you found someone else? Is that it?"

"What?"

115

"Like Alison did to you. Have you met someone better?"

"God, No!"

"I thought you said you loved me. What did I do wrong?"

"Tilly don't do this. There is nothing wrong with you at all. You are a fabulous, warm-hearted, hard-working woman that some lucky guy is going to want to spend the rest of his life with." She looked away.

"I can't be the one to break your spirit, Tilly."

They fell into a silence, punctuated with the occasional sob from Tilly, after which Joe would squeeze her hand.

When they pulled up to her house, they sat still in the car for a long time.

"Is your dad home?"

"His car is here, so probably."

"Tilly, I have to do this."

"I know."

Tilly got out of Joe's car and let herself into the house. Her arms and legs were heavy. As she trailed upstairs, she shouted out,

"Dad, Dad? Joe needs to talk to you."

"What the hell? Tilly? Shit, if this is my fault, I'll …"

Max went outside to talk to Joe. Tilly could see them from her window. She couldn't hear what they were saying, but neither looked happy. Max turned and glanced up at her in the window. Joe's eyes followed. When he saw her standing at the window, he turned away and walked back to his car. Max followed him.

The men shook hands, and Joe got back into his car and drove away.

Tilly heard her dad coming up the stairs, so she dived into her bathroom to wash her face.

"Tilly?"

"In here, dad."

"Are you all right?"

"Yes, I'm fine,"

"Now why don't I believe that?"

With a deep breath, Tilly came out of the bathroom to find her dad sitting on her bed. He patted the space next to him.

"The guy is going through something, Tilly. From what James said last week, he is improving, but they think it's going to take some time. It's probably best to walk away from this one. You have a new job. Why not focus on that for now?"

"Dad!"

"Tilly, listen, I am not telling you to marry someone else tomorrow. I am saying, just for the time being, concentrate on work, focus on what you want to do."

"Thanks, dad."

"So, are you ready to win this tournament on Thursday?"

Chapter Twenty One

On Sunday, Tilly got up slowly and then rang Emily.

"We need to work on Plan B. Meet me at Hollywood Bowl."

"Tilly, why not walk away?"

"How long have you known me?"

"I get that this might be a new concept for you Tilly, but if this guy needs space. Maybe you should do just that. Let him have the space?"

"You are probably right, but doing well in this tournament will feel a lot better than coming last. Besides, he isn't even going to be there on Thursday."

"I didn't think you were playing?"

"Technically, I'm not, but I have this awful feeling Mrs Trench will not join in. She will make some excuse, then sit and tut in the background."

During the next three working days, Tilly crossed every T and dotted every I. She had all the shirts steamed and hung ready. The bowling alley was keen to make this upgraded version of their usual events work, so they pulled out all the stops, too.

When Thursday came, she was ready. Max had decided they should all travel to the event as a family. Alex joined them for breakfast.

"I got a text this morning from Angela."

"Angela?"

"Janet's assistant. It seems Mrs Trench won't make it today. She has to go to the emergency dentist." Tilly let out a long breath and sank onto a chair.

"I was wondering what excuse she would use," huffed Max.

"Looks like you get to play after all Tills. Are you coming with us, mum?"

"Not this morning, son. Lynne and I are off on a bonding session of our own, but we will be there in the afternoon."

"Good! You will be there in time to present James and me with our trophies then." Max smiled at his wife.

"I hope so because I have those five extra days of holiday already planned."

Tilly finally spoke. "Sorry, do you mean Janet will not be there at all? But she won't see all the work I have done."

"Don't worry, sweetheart. It will probably be easier this way. Now she can't steal all your glory, either."

At the Hollywood Bowl Centre, Tilly was impressed with how things were looking. They used company pop-up banners all around to create a section for them. Alternate screens above the lanes had the Sykes International and JMC technology logos on.

Tilly had done a deal with the centre, so they had left extra lanes free to give them some privacy. Jugs of beer and soft drinks were ready on the tables. She had people's names printed on their team shirts and matching drink cups.

Tilly was excited to meet Joanne as she would be the first person she had met from JMC that wasn't called Cookson. She hoped she was a 'pink girl' as that was the shirt colour Emily had suggested would set off her colouring the best. Tilly wasn't sure, she rarely wore pink. Her hope was the green flashes and writing would work for her.

Leaving Alex to sort out the team from Sykes International, Tilly was greeting the people from JMC. The first four were there and trying on their shirts, but there was no sign of her partner Joanne or the Cooksons.

Tilly had butterflies in her stomach. Her games on Sunday had been hit and miss, but the long chat had been most useful. By the end of the day, she realised this was not the time to be chasing Joe Cookson. Space. Everyone kept saying he needed space, and that was what she was going to do. She had a new job, and she needed to settle back into life, living with her parents after university. That was enough for now. Thank goodness for good friends. Today, she had plenty of other things to think about.

Alex came bouncing up to her. His shirt was black with red flashes and writing. It looked great with his black jeans and Tilly knew Patrick would look good in it, too.

"So, where's my partner? Do you think he is any good?"

"I get the impression he is competitive, and I think Joe once said he admires dad's drive."

"What time do we start?"

"Ten minutes ago!"

"Argh! I'll go ask if anyone from JMC has heard anything."

As people came into the centre, Tilly was searching for Joanne. She thought she would recognise her easily, as she was sure she was a curvy girl based on her shirt and shoe size. She was also watching Alex talking to the people from JMC, who were all checking their phones and shaking their heads.

It was a full thirty minutes after the start time when the Cooksons arrived. All of them. Tilly was not expecting to see Joe and was surprised at how much her body reacted when she saw him in the group. There was always something physical about her reaction to him. Nothing in her history prepared her for the feeling she felt seeing him walking reluctantly behind his brothers.

Michael rushed over to Tilly, full of apologies.

"I'm sorry. I hope we haven't cocked up the programme too much."

"It all depends on how fast we play the pool games, but I'm sure it will all work out."

"I hope so, because my mother insisted we bring my baby brother."

"Oh!" was all she could manage to say as Joe came to stand next to his brother. Michael slapped him on the back.

"So Tilly, may I present your partner for the day, 'Jo Hansom'." Michael was enjoying this embarrassment.

"Oh!" Tilly had to find more words.

Joe was looking bedraggled again. As always, his clothes were clean. It was the beard that gave him away.

For the first three frames, Tilly was walking through the process in a dream. She wished so much to spend time with Joe again. After the weekend and Emily's pep talk, she hadn't wanted to think about when that would happen. She was sure it was too soon for Plan B and was worried that anything she might say would push them further apart.

Tilly and Joe were playing a team from both R & D departments. Their opponents were chatting away and seemed to be getting to know each other. That is what she wanted; it was what her dad wanted. Tilly couldn't stand the silence any longer.

"Why are you here?"

"Do you think I want to be?"

"So?"

"Well, it began with the mums. When your mum arrived this morning, she made a big fuss and wanted to meet me. So, my mum made me get dressed!"

"Then one by one they started. First, it was moaning that I hadn't worked my notice."

"You haven t been going to work?"

"I haven't been going anywhere."

"You made an exception to dump me."

"Tilly!" She stood up to take her turn, leaving Joe steaming.

Tilly sat back down, inhaling the minty spice she would always associate with Joe.

"Would you have preferred I sent a text?" He hissed.

"No." It was an empty voice, but Tilly was past hiding her hurt.

"Dad said today was about family, that we needed to pull together." He shook his head. "And your mother just sat there staring at me."

"Hmm, she's quite good at that… I'm sorry."

Joe took his turn and when he bowled a spare, they edged into the lead. Tilly felt a little bit of hope until Joe sat down again, looking resigned.

"That was good Joe, how do you do that?"

"It's all about angles, really." The silence was back, and Tilly hated it.

"So, the parents ganged up on you, eh?"

"Well, they managed to make me feel guilty."

"And that made you turn up?"

"No, that was when Patrick and Michael arrived to pick dad up." He grimaced. "Seems they heard you were coming as a family, so dad said we should do the same."

Max and James were playing on the next lane. They both turned and looked directly at their youngest children. Tilly nudged Joe and nodding pointed out their audience.

"It's going to be like that all day, isn't it?"

She had been playing mechanically with most of her brain focusing on the tournament and if the late start would cause a problem at lunchtime. She was worried about what to say to Joe, so she said very little. From what he said earlier, and the state of his beard, Tilly guessed he had been moping around the house again. The last thing she wanted to do was to make it worse.

With two frames to go, the team from R & D had started to pull back. Joe squeezed her hand. Tilly blushed. He leaned in to speak into her ear.

"You are going to need to up your game if we are going to win."

"Sorry, I have a lot on my mind."

"Michael said today was important to you."

"They were all picking on you this morning."

"Michael started on me last week. In fact, he said nothing today." He squeezed her hand again. "Just watch me."

Tilly tried to work out what Joe was doing differently. He seemed to consistently get all the pins down with his two balls.

"I still don't know how to play any better than before I watched you."

"Look at that screen, see, it's telling you where to aim."

"Where?"

"The blue arrow."

"Is that what that is?"

The R & D team were whispering and scribbling things on scraps of paper.

"One last frame Tilly. We need to win this one."

"You're just making me nervous."

"Sorry, babe." He threw his arm across her shoulder and pulled her into his side.

"I don't think that's going to help."

"I don't know. It looks like it's distracting everyone else. Your dad just dropped a ball."

"Oh well, who am I to argue?" She stood up and kissed Joe on the cheek. She took her time and managed to get eight pins. It was her best score so far. When Joe knocked down all 10 pins and then 8 with his extra ball, they had won their first game. Joe hugged Tilly, lifting her off the ground.

"We did it, Tilly, we did it." Tilly was happy. Her idea for the event looked to be a success, and Joe was talking to her. The smile on her face was so wide.

"Does this mean we are friends again?"

"I can't imagine ever not wanting to be your friend Matilda Sykes."

Their second game was easier, and Joe tried to help Tilly as much as he could. Tilly was more relaxed because things seemed to be going well. Talking to Joe had become easier, too.

Their final game of the morning was against their fathers.

"This is like some surreal nightmare. I feel I'm jousting to win your hand in marriage."

"Not that two kings are trying to marry off their kids to cement peace between two warring countries."

"Whose idea was this?"

"Mine, hang on I need to check something about lunch." Tilly pulled a bulging folder out of her bag getting a paper cut in the process.

"You're very retro, aren't you? I expected everything to be on your phone." Tilly was sucking her finger to control the bleeding. She pulled the finger out of her mouth with a pop.

"Shit signal when I was here last week." She muttered, then went back to sucking her finger. Joe pulled it out of her mouth.

"Here. Let me look." He produced a handkerchief and wrapped it around her finger, using pressure to stop the bleeding.

"Keep that for your collection." Tilly beamed a smile at him, and Joe could not stop himself from hugging her.

"Oh! Tilly." Coughs from their opponents stopped them from going any further.

"Is this how you win – inappropriate touching – putting the other team off?"

"Is it working?"

"It's making me wonder why you have been holed up in your bedroom for two weeks."

Joe shrugged and made his score count. STRIKE.

It was Joe's turn to smile and Tilly's chance to hug him.

"I protest!"

"Sorry, dad."

"Well, we liked it." The mothers had arrived in time to eat with the rest.

"I'm guessing lunch is late because we held things up getting Joe here." Lynne sounded happy.

"It looks like that effort was worth it." Carole Sykes nudged her husband.

"I'm not so sure!" Max growled.

The match on their lane was the last one to finish. The other players gathered around to watch their final frame.

Tilly and Joe had already done enough to win, but having a crowd meant Tilly's nerves were showing again. Her first attempt went straight into the gutter. As she waited for her ball to return, Joe stood and calmly whispered into her ear.

"Close your eyes, Tilly. Block them out and 'concentrate on the lane. Focus on that front pin." Joe's voice filled her body. This was the last ball of the morning. If she hit one pin, they would win their pool. Tilly stopped and took a deep breath. She could smell and feel Joe. The pervading sense of being home filled her body. Another deep breath that she let out slowly. She shut out all the other voices. Stepping slowly up to the lane, she let the ball go. Nine pins fell. Joe lifted her from behind and spun her around. They were through to the final to play Patrick and Alex.

She was with Joe. They were together, if only for this event.

Chapter Twenty Two

They ate lunch in the retro diner. Burger, fries, and shakes. Emily had helped Tilly create a fun menu with names that linked the two companies. Tilly sat with Alex and the Cookson brothers at a table set in a vintage American car.

"I feel like I am at a kid's birthday party. Is there a cake?"

"Cheesecake!" Tilly's eyes lit up.

"My little sister here always wants cheesecake for her birthday cake, so I started doing the same. But between you and me, our mum couldn't bake. She would try every year to make a birthday cake, but when Tills asked for a cheesecake, she gave in and bought one."

It made Tilly glance over to the table where the parents were also tucking into burgers and fries. They were all talking with their hands and Tilly hoped it was all good. She caught her dad's eye, and he smiled.

"I have to hand it to you Tilly; this is way more fun than the normal events we get to go to with work. Hell, even Grumpy is smiling."

"I hate to break it to you, Michael, I don't think it's the cheeseburgers that have put the smile on his face."

"He did always enjoy bowling."

"Thank you. I wanted to bring in some changes and get people talking."

Patrick had been quiet. He seemed to focus on his meal and checking out what was happening around the diner. He lifted his head and stared at Michael.

"If Joe wins this thing, I am not sure I will forgive you for orchestrating his appearance."

All eyes fell on Michael. Waiting for an explanation. Tilly remembered Joe saying that he had said nothing that morning. She tried reprocessing all the conversations she had with Michael around today. Eventually, she settled on the message to her dad about Joanne Hansom.

"Joanne Hansom?"

"It's a nickname we used for him when we were younger, his hair was often longer. We tormented him about being a girl and called him Joanne."

"So, you knew he would be coming when you messaged my dad?" Michael nodded.

"Who else knew?" Michael looked round the room.

"Everyone, I guess, except you and him, that is."

"Alex?"

"I didn't really understand it. Dad tried to tell me, but I kept getting confused over who knew, so I didn't dare ask anyone to explain."

Joe stood up from the table and silently walked away.

"Shit! Mum will kill me if he goes back to growing that beard."

"Why Michael? Just why?" Tilly couldn't hide her feelings. Her body rigid, her anger clear in her voice. Michael held up his hands in surrender.

"We thought it would be awkward for us as families if you guys weren't speaking. Mum got super worried he wouldn't pull out of it this time. I only did as I was told."

"Do you think someone should go explain that to him?" Across the room, Lynne Cookson got out of her chair and once more followed her son out of the building. Tilly watched on from the seat that had somehow welded itself to her legs.

It took her a while to realise she had things to do to get ready for the afternoon. Once she had worked out who was playing who in the playoff, she entered the names on the score sheets. Now the teams could find which lane they were on.

Her big worry became what would happen with the final against Alex and Patrick. That was the climax of the event and if Joe didn't come back, it would end the day on a sour note.

Three lanes were in use. Tilly stood with her mum and Alex as they waited to hear from Lynne. Patrick had gone outside to see if he could see them or at least get a phone signal to call his mum.

It took thirty minutes for him to return.

"Mum's got him. They are on their way back." Patrick disappeared toward the toilets once he had delivered the news.

Carole Sykes put her arm around her daughter. Tilly offered her a weak smile.

"It will be OK, sweetheart. It is all going so well."

"He has been in a bad place, mum. He has been hurt so much already."

"Watch your dad. He is so enjoying this."

"Mum!"

"I'm just trying to get you to see the positives. Oh, here's Lynne and Joe. How do you want to play this?"

Tilly scanned the faces of Lynne and Joe; she knew Lynne would let her know what to do. When Lynne's head moved in the smallest of nods, Tilly took her cue and went over to talk to them.

"I've explained that I was the one who put pressure on everyone else to make this happen. I am sorry I didn't tell you Tilly, but I wasn't sure you wouldn't tell him."

"Joe, are you OK to finish this? I'll understand if you don't."

"Matilda Sykes, if I mess up your day, I know you will make me suffer."

"You have a point." She held out her hand for Joe to shake. He took her hand and pulled her into a big hug.

"Come on, we have to show these people who they are messing with. Friends?"

"Friends."

"Right, come over here. I have stuff to teach you if we are going to beat those two."

Chapter Twenty Three

When the time came for the last match, the rest of the group gathered around. The tables were filled with more jugs of beer and nachos. Lynne and Carole sat to one side with a jug of cocktails.

Joe put his arm around Tilly and pulled her close. His forehead against hers. He spoke softly into her ear.

"Look, everyone is enjoying this. You have done so well. You realise the rest of JMC will be happy to see Patrick lose this final. I need you to do everything I say."

"So, you are back and taking this seriously?"

"Don't you want to win?"

"Like you, I am playing my big brother. Do you know how often I have won anything against him?"

"Probably about as many times as I have won against Patrick."

"I will try my hardest. You can count on that, but I am simply thrilled that it's going well, and people are talking to each other."

"And I'm happy that we can talk." He rubbed her arm. "We can be friends, can't we Tilly? I don't like the idea that we can't."

"I think that is the best bit."

With everyone else standing up to watch the final, Tilly felt a different type of nervousness. The event was a success, measured simply by the fact people were chatting with each other and they all seemed to be enjoying themselves.

The expression on her father's face gave Tilly a warm glow, but when Joe squeezed her hand, she coloured up.

As he leaned in to whisper, she felt his breath on the delicate skin by her ear.

"This will not be a straightforward game, babe. Patrick is good at anything like this."

"So, we do our best, right?"

"Let's see what happens when I do this?" And he kissed her neck and slipped an arm around her shoulder. Tilly's face was ablaze. She lowered her gaze.

"Joe, are you sure? Everyone is watching, not just Alex and Patrick."

"I guess we could have fun with this. What do you think?" Tilly searched his face, looking long into his eyes. Her brain scrambled to protect her from believing this was real.

"I think I better go to the toilet before this game gets started."

Tilly locked the stall door and pulled out her phone.

Tilly: Shit shit shit!

Em: What happened?

Tilly: Joe turned up and is my partner!

Em: So, Plan B is in play. How's it going?

Tilly: We have agreed to be friends.

Em: oh, the friend zone.

Tilly: Now he wants to do lots of PDA to put the other team off.

Em: Oh!

Tilly: We are playing Alex and his brother, it's the final.

Em: Hmmm.

Tilly: Which means everyone is watching.

Em: So, we are in the middle of Plan B, and he wants you to do the pretend boyfriend thing? Sounds like the guy just scored a home goal.

Tilly: I look like a beetroot though.

Em: Get out there and show him what being Matilda Sykes' boyfriend could really mean.

Tilly: Are you sure?

Em: Go for it, girl.

Tilly took the time to brush her hair and redo her lip gloss. Then, with one last peep in the mirror, she returned to the lanes to stake her claim on Joe Cookson. She walked straight up to him and threw her arms around his neck and gave him a big kiss. The sort of kiss that says this is my guy, hands off. Joe took a split second to respond. But when he did, he was full-on into it. His arms went around her waist as he pulled her hard into his body. When the kiss ended, he peppered tiny kisses across to her ear.

"I guess that is a yes, then?"

"I think we better sit down, though."

"This is going to be fun."

The first few frames were tight, but Tilly could see Alex was locking agitated when she found an excuse to touch Joe. She found she wanted to touch him more and more. For his part, Joe kept calling her Babe and made a point of kissing her every time he sat down after his go.

He spent a lot of time whispering in her ear. Tilly's body was a jumble of sensations, but it was the intimacy of Joe's mouth on or near the delicate skin on her neck that seem to affect her the most. Each time she stood up to take her turn, she had to close her eyes and stop to find her centre again. She had a sneaking feeling that this was probably affecting them more than it was affecting Alex and Patrick.

Joe's scores continued to be big ones, and although she was improving, Alex and Patrick were still in the lead.

"We need you to be scoring another two on each frame. I want you to watch me this time."

Tilly had trouble watching Joe collecting his ball, approaching the lane, and releasing it. She studied every inch of his body. The way the muscles and tendons in his forearm moved, how he took a stance, and the way his face changed through the process. STRIKE.

She was so excited, she stood up to hug him again. Joe lifted her into his arms and spun her around. Over Joe's shoulder, she saw her dad's face twist into a smirk. *What has amused my dad? Dare I ask him?*

Joe's strike had edged them back into the lead. Whilst Alex was bowling, Joe put his arm around Tilly and tickled her.

"Having fun Babe?"

"Yes, are you glad you came back?"

"Yes, I am. I am enjoying this?"

"Which 'this' exactly?"

135

"Being with you." Tilly thought she would melt onto the floor.

Alex was not happy at all. He scored a grand total of one on that turn. He looked at Tilly, obviously annoyed, but Tilly wasn't sure why. Was it because he was losing or because he didn't like what was happening to his sister? Max came over and whispered to him as he sat down. Tilly was surprised when Alex smiled at whatever their dad was saying. Tilly could see Alex studying her closely. It unnerved her just a little. Maybe her dad realised it was a tactic between her and Joe. And with that thought came the realisation that it was only a game, and they would still be parting when this match was over.

Tilly stood frozen at the end of the lane, her ball hanging at her side. Suddenly, Joe was behind her, his arms around her waist.

Leaning forward, he kissed the top of her head.

"What's wrong Babe?"

"I think I forgot we were only pretending, and I don't want this to end, Joe."

"I know what you mean."

"Really?"

"Tilly, are you going to play that ball?"

"In a minute!" she snapped back at Patrick, and she put the ball back on the rack. Turning, she spoke quietly to Joe. "So why? Why does it have to be over?"

"Well, I don't want to hurt you and our families?"

"Really! Really! What are you going to do to hurt me, Joe?"

"Well, nothing. I would never want to hurt you." Tilly, in full flow now, turned to address the room, her arms folded across her chest. Everyone watched them intently. Even people playing on the other lanes.

"Is there anybody here who has a problem with me going out with Joe?" Dropping her hands to her hips, she looked around, searching their faces. Her mum smiled. Lynne Cookson beamed. Certainly, neither of them seemed to have an issue.

"Alex?"

"Well, no."

Eventually, Tilly looked squarely at her dad and lifted her eyebrow in question. Maxwell Sykes laughed and shook his head no.

Happy with the response, Tilly collected her ball again. She approached the lane with a sense of purpose and released her ball. STRIKE!

With two frames to go, it looked like Joe and Tilly could actually win. Alex and Patrick were scoring well, but Tilly and Joe were on fire. Tilly was the last person to bowl. Her first ball rolled into the gutter.

"It's OK Babe, you know what to do. You just need to hit three. Hit three and we win those extra five days' holiday, and I will take you back to Portofino."

Tilly smiled she could do this. She pulled back her arm, but as the ball came through, she caught her leg. The ball dropped to the floor and rolled down toward the pins at a snail's pace. Silence had descended on the crowd again.

The ball rolled to the left and managed to hit one pin before it slid out the side. The group erupted as Patrick and Alex jumped up and down.

Joe rushed over to Tilly. She wondered what he was going to say. She had lost the game and the extra holiday. To her surprise, he hugged her hard.

"You were wonderful Babe."

"But we lost?"

"But that speech, I think we won more than a plastic trophy."

"And the holiday?"

"Tilly, do we need to be on holiday to be happy?"

"No Joe, if we are together, then I really don't care where we are."

A note from the author

I hope you enjoyed reading When Joe Met Matilda. They started as a couple already formed in the first Love Comes With The Job novel Batting For Charlie.

I hope you enjoy reading it if you haven't read it already. The next Love Comes With the Job story is Presenting With Daniel. I hope to have news of its release very soon.

Come and find me on Facebook too and join the group Love Love Books, a wonderful place for romance readers to hang out and share stories and of course hear about new releases from me and other authors.

Printed in Great Britain
by Amazon

21084860R00080